To Dye For
An Isabel and Alma Trumbo Cozy Mystery

Ed Lynskey

Other Books by Ed Lynskey

Isabel and Alma Trumbo Cozy Mystery Series
Quiet Anchorage
The Cashmere Shroud
The Ladybug Song
The Amber Top Hat
Sweet Betsy
Murder in a One-Hearse Town
Vi's Ring
Heirloom
A Big Dill
Eve's Win
To Dye For

Piper and Bill Robins Cozy Mystery Series
The Corpse Wore Gingham
Fur the Win

Hope Jones Cozy Mystery Series (as Lyn Key)
Nozy Cat 1
Nozy Cat 2
Nozy Cat 3
Nozy Cat 4

Ginny Dove Cozy Mystery Series (as Lea Charles)
Found Key
Easy Peasy
No Picnic

Juno Patchen Cozy Mystery Series
Berried Truth
Berried Past
Berried Lies

Private Investigator Frank Johnson Mystery Series
Pelham Fell Here
The Dirt-Brown Derby
The Blue Cheer
Troglodytes
The Zinc Zoo
After the Big Noise

Chapter 1

"Petey Samson is pitching a barking fit." Tall and lean, Isabel was the older Trumbo sister in her spry seventies. "I'd better go check on him."

"He's acted so devilish lately." Short and rotund, Alma was the two-years-younger Trumbo sister. They relaxed sitting in the living room poring over the morning newspaper, sipping chicory coffee, and sharing town gossip.

Isabel went into the kitchen. Their butterball of a beagle wagged his tail and peered up at her with his soulful brown eyes. He was eager to get his reward for looking cute as a button, and he knew she was a pushover. The empty doggie treats packet sat by the broken toaster where Alma had doled out the last one. They recorded any item they ran out of on the grocery-shopping list magnetized to the refrigerator. However, Alma had grown derelict in her duties, and Isabel feared another sister's tiff was brewing.

"What ails you, pooch?" Isabel asked.

Woof-woof.

"Sorry, but we've run out of doggie treats."

Woof-woof.

"Why is he so keyed up?" Alma stopped beside Isabel.

"Somebody dispensed the last doggie treat and didn't add it to the grocery-shopping list."

"I swear you're turning so forgetful. Have you thought of taking ginkgo biloba tablets?"

"You left the empty doggie treats packet on the counter."

"So I did. We'll have to go grocery shopping then."

Isabel detected Alma's cagey undertone. "Since we're out anyway, we may as well make a pit stop at Eddy's Deli."

"If you insist on it, by all means, let's do it."

Woof-woof.

"Of course we'll take you," Isabel said. "Don't we always?"

"How does he know we just discussed a shopping trip?"

"All I know is our household is going to the dogs where our lives revolve around this one."

"My, aren't we a little sunbeam this morning?"

Isabel had a wistful sigh. "We haven't tackled a mystery in ages, and I get crabby if I don't have one to engage me."

Alma nodded. "I thought as much. You've got it bad."

"It's not just me. You've been cantankerous as a bag of badgers."

"Face it, Isabel. The same sleuthing bug curses us both."

"We're turning into a pair of old fuddy-duddies."

"Bite your tongue. Fuddy-duddy isn't in our lexicon."

"Stopping by and saying hello to Sheriff Fox will perk up our spirits. He's probably forgotten how our faces look."

"Rumor has it he thumbtacked up our photos beside his wanted posters and throws darts at them."

"I'm heartened to hear we still mean so much to him."

A bebop jazz instrumental struck up. Looking for its source, Alma scanned the kitchen. She didn't put stock in ghosts, and even if she did, she doubted if they could play a saxophone and trumpet so masterfully. When she glanced at Isabel, she winked.

"My new ringtone is Coltrane and Miles."

"They never played together any smoother and tighter. Where is your smartphone?"

"I stash it in the broken toaster for safekeeping."

"Safekeeping?"

"I keep misplacing it, so I thought of the toaster. Isn't it a stroke of genius?"

"It's a good thing the toaster is broken."

Woof-woof.

"Okay, I'll answer it. Give me half a chance. Jeez, we're such an uptight bunch today."

Isabel extracted her smartphone and answered its ring.

"Sheriff Fox here, Isabel. How are you this morning?"

Isabel put on her speakerphone. "Get to the point. Has there been another one?"

"Yes ma'am. Murder has reared its gory head again," Sheriff Fox replied. "You and Alma are the only townies who are happy to hear the bad news."

"Utter poppycock and balderdash. We're never happy to learn of a town murder, but you confront a new perplexing whodunit," Isabel said. "Do you seek our proven expertise?"

"No, I'm calling to invite you over for Earl Gray tea and lemon drizzle scones," Sheriff Fox replied. "Afterward, we can play croquet and badminton on the town lawn."

"You're having a bad day, and I get that," Isabel said. "However, your snarky remarks serve no gainful purpose. Who died from the foul play?"

"Laura Isherwood," Sheriff Fox replied.

"She works--I mean she worked--at Farrah's Beauty Shop," Isabel said, closing her eyes and shaking her head.

Alma, shuddering in horror, sent up a silent prayer for the departed's final rest and peace.

"Laura was a hairstylist employed here," Sheriff Fox said.

"Who discovered her?" Isabel asked.

"Farrah called it in to me," Sheriff Fox replied. "How soon will I see you and Alma?"

"We haven't gotten dressed, taken down our hair rollers, or walked Petey Samson," Isabel replied.

"You'll be tied up for the next hour." Sheriff Fox was annoyed.

Isabel smiled. "Are you timing us? Is it a race? Laura isn't going anywhere."

"Actually, she's due shortly for taking a one-way trip to the morgue," Sheriff Fox said. "Can you make it snappy?"

"Ladies at our golden ages don't do snappy, but we'll not poke along," Isabel replied. "Bye for now."

"Are you any happier now?" Alma asked.

"My heartbeats are pounding like a woodpecker drumming on a hollow gum tree." Isabel placed her hand over it. "Imagine a woman of my vintage experiencing an adrenaline rush."

"I hope I can remember where I left my sleuth hat," Alma said.

"You can borrow one of mine," Isabel said. "My closet shelf is filled with them."

"It's Petey Samson's naptime," Alma said.

"He's already left us to curl up on my bed," Isabel said.

"Don't forget to tuck him in with his little blanket and pillow," Alma said.

"He's spoiled rotten to the core," Isabel said.

"Happiness is spoiling a pet rotten to the core," Alma said.

Main Street in Quiet Anchorage, Virginia, had undergone a few subtle changes since Isabel and Alma grew up decades ago on the Trumbo family farm located just outside of town. The post office had moved down the block to the larger facility, and an antique shop operated there now. The town council had voted to install the new streetlights resembling old gas lamps, and the merchants preserved the pastel colors, brass doorknobs, and rustic architecture.

Farrah had established her beauty shop about the same time Isabel and Alma had retired and moved back to Quiet Anchorage. Both sisters were customers. However, they booked their hair appointments at different times so they could glean more town chitchat. Fussier about how she looked, Isabel's hair appointments also took longer than Alma's did. They hadn't visited the beauty shop together until this morning.

Sheriff Roscoe Fox, fidgety and bleary-eyed, met them at the door. A paunchy six-footer, he wore his Smokey Bear uniform hat to cover his bald spot. He was astute enough to know using his lady sleuths on a homicide investigation made his job a darn sight easier, and he always strove to make things easier.

"Where have you been piddling around?" Sheriff Fox asked. "I just finished my work and sent back my CSI folks."

"Good morning to you as well," Isabel replied.

"We've also had an eventful morning," Alma said. "First we fished Isabel's ringing smartphone out of the toaster."

"I only put bread slices in mine," Sheriff Fox said.

"Then we hit the grocery market and bought Petey Samson's doggie treats," Alma said.

"The poor dear has had to do without them," Isabel said.

"I've never known anybody who pampers their mutt as much as you ladies do," Sheriff Fox said.

"We think he's more than worth it," Alma said.

"Murder is our present focus," Sheriff Fox said.

"We haven't forgotten," Isabel said.

Isabel surveyed the row of six salon styling chairs placed before the styling station mirrors. Blow dryers, scissors, combs, brushes, and curling irons lay on each station table. A hairspray face shield lay on one station table. The coffee bar off to the side offered the customers cups of hot cocoa, espresso, and tea while they waited. On Friday mornings, Farrah also brought in and set out boxes of doughnuts or pastries.

The advertisements for hair products appeared on the ceiling tiles for the customers to read while lying horizontally in the reclining chairs at the shampoo sinks. The easy-listening jazz--but no Coltrane and Miles--piped in created a laid-back vibe. Isabel fingered her center-parted gray hair, debating if she needed to make her next hair appointment sooner.

Usually abuzz with the customers' bright chatter and banter, the beauty shop was now a quiet if not depressing ghost town. Murder disrupted business. The hairstylists returned home after Farrah shut down her operations. Hopefully, it didn't drag on for too long. The ladies needed to look their elegant finest. Anything less was unacceptable and created an epic crisis.

Isabel cringed at hearing the grandfather clock by the check-in desk chiming out its resonating *bing-bong, bing-bong* eight times. Farrah cherished the grandfather clock, which still kept accurate time. Watching its heavy pendulum rod and bob constructed of brass swinging back and forth left Isabel dizzy.

She wasn't a big fan. Hearing the grandfather clock mark the fleeting passage of time--*tick-tock, tick-tock*--was unnerving and eerie in an Edgar Allan Poe sort of way. She'd stick with consulting her smartphone or wristwatch if she wished to know the time. Besides, their cramped living room had no niche for moving in a bulky six-foot-tall grandfather clock.

"Where is Farrah?" Isabel asked. "Did you send her home?"

"She's down at the station house," Sheriff Fox replied.

Isabel eyed him warily. "Surely, you haven't arrested her for Laura Isherwood's murder."

"Farrah is giving her written statement to Deputy Sheriff Bexley," Sheriff Fox said. "She's upset and said she couldn't do it while she was in here this morning."

"Her feelings are still understandably fresh and raw," Isabel said.

Alma scoped out the floor. "Where did you find Laura's dead body?"

"She lay sprawled out on the floor by her station chair," Sheriff Fox replied. "I took dozens of crime scene photos if you need to review them."

"How did she die besides tragically?" Isabel asked.

"Her assailant struck her in the temple with a blunt solid object," Sheriff Fox replied.

"Did you recover it?" Isabel asked. "Could we be so blessed this time?"

"I looked everywhere but no dice." Sheriff Fox nudged back the Smokey Bear hat and scratched his forehead. "Laura's killer probably took it while exiting the premises."

"Perhaps so," Isabel said. "Why did Laura arrive here before Farrah got in?"

"She said Laura came in early to open up," Sheriff Fox replied.

"So, she trusted Laura enough to give her a door key," Isabel said.

"You make a reasonable assumption," Sheriff Fox said.

"Have you found anything akin to a clue or lead?" Isabel asked.

"Nothing so far has come to light," Sheriff Fox replied. "However, something useful will soon turn up." Thumbs hooked in his gun belt, he chuckled. "The perfect murder is impossible to pull off, after all." Again, he chuckled.

"Says who?" Isabel didn't chuckle.

"Says you is who," Sheriff Fox replied.

"Alma and I would never make such a haughty claim," Isabel said. "The FBI says 40% of homicide cases go cold and remain unsolved for decades if they ever are solved."

Sheriff Fox's humor vanished. "Isabel, I hope what you just said doesn't lower a voodoo hex on us. The mayor urges me to make a timely arrest, or she'll blow her stack, fire me, and appoint an acting town sheriff."

Tapping her chin, Isabel smiled while she relished the possibility.

"Now see here, Isabel. I resent your show of disloyalty," Sheriff Fox said. "We've got a good thing going, and you don't want to throw a monkey wrench into the works."

Isabel nodded. "We'll stick to our usual game plan and hope for the best outcome."

"That sounds more like it," Sheriff Fox said. "Where is Sammi Jo? Why isn't she with you? I expect to see all hands on deck at a critical time like this."

"She's on vacation this week, but she doesn't give us a daily schedule of her activities," Isabel replied.

"Who else can you use as your backup?" Sheriff Fox asked.

"Our next best option is the Three Musketeers," Isabel replied.

"Are they occupying the liars' bench?" Sheriff Fox asked.

"Some mornings take them a tad bit longer to get started," Isabel replied. "If you should ever reach the ripe old age of eighty plus, you'll understand what I mean."

"I plan on being the town sheriff for at least that long," Sheriff Fox said.

"I wouldn't be trumpeting your long-range plans," Isabel said. "Taking it one day at a time is a more sensible approach, especially while you're investigating Laura's murder."

"How soon can you give me the killer's name?" Sheriff Fox asked.

Isabel glanced at her smartphone. "It's been ten minutes since we arrived, so I'll go out on a limb by saying it'll take us at least until the day's end, probably longer, to know anything."

"I'm declaring it a code red priority," Sheriff Fox said.

"Rest assured we'll give it our closest attention," Isabel said.

"However, we tend to plod along at our own deliberate pace so bear with us," Alma said.

"The same ground rules apply." Sheriff Fox squinted as he pointed at them. "I want to know about every clue or lead in real time as you uncover it. I forbid your under-the-table meddling. You need the proper oversight only I can give you. Am I clear?"

"Whatever you say," Alma replied.

"We must remain in close communication as we move forward," Sheriff Fox said.

Alma couldn't help but smile when Isabel slipped her a coy wink.

Chapter 2

"You promised me that we'd stop at Eddy's Deli," Alma said.

Isabel pursed her lips in exasperation as she drove down Main Street in their blue four-door sedan.

"Alma, you have a one-track mind," Isabel said. "All I hear from you is my bear claws this and my bear claws that. Can't you put them out of your mind?"

"I know we're back on the case. Nonetheless, I have to satisfy my sweet tooth, so it doesn't distract me like it's doing now."

Isabel thought of something just as, if not more, important to Alma as her bear claws, a flaky, sweet pastry topped with sliced almonds and raisins served at Eddy's Deli.

"Didn't I notice on the wall calendar your next hair appointment is scheduled later on this week?" Isabel asked.

"Yes, it is," Alma replied. "So what?"

"Wasn't Laura also your hairstylist?"

"You know she took care of both of our hair needs."

"She certainly won't now. Who'll be our new hairstylist?"

"We'll ask Farrah for her recommendation."

"Farrah is distraught and in no shape to reopen her beauty shop much less give us a hairstylist recommendation. We have to track down the murderer, so she can put this tragedy behind her, call in her hairstylists, and set up shop to coif our tresses again."

"In the interim, we'll have to trek the seven miles to Warrenton for a haircut. I hate making the long drive."

"We should identify our first murder suspect before we do anything else."

Alma gave a slow nod. "Laura's inner circle is a good place to start. Was she married? She and I talked about the townies, but she never told me a whole lot about her personal life."

"I happen to know her husband's name is Deacon. His photo ran in the newspaper last summer. He posed with Blaine Matthiessen behind a trophy fish they'd landed while fishing in the Cornet River."

"Blaine can tell us his fish story," Alma said.

"The fish probably gets larger each time he repeats it," Isabel said.

Stepping through the doorway of the town hardware store transported Isabel back to her girlhood. Of the three Trumbo sisters, she was the handiest with tools to make farm repairs. She breathed in the resinous fragrance of turpentine as they maneuvered down the aisle cluttered with kitchenware, light bulbs, and Ball Mason canning jars. The light-grained wood floor was maple like the floors she saw in bowling alleys, school gyms, and ballet halls.

"Well, I'll be a suck-egg mule on the Fourth of July." Blaine leaned on the push broom handle. "Isabel and Alma are in the house. If I didn't know any better, I'd say they're investigating the Laura Isherwood murder. We have our town private eyes."

Isabel smiled at the behemoth of a young man who'd played defensive tackle on the high school football team (the entire town shut down for the games). His easygoing nature, casual humor, and toothy grin won him a legion of friends. He must've stuffed his armoire with denim bib overalls since he seldom varied his attire. His steel-toe work boots ran a size 15 while the horny calluses toughened his leathery palms. He wasn't afraid of physical labor, and he pitched in if anybody asked him for his assistance. Folks said he was dating an earnest-minded young lady, and his bachelor days were dwindling even if he seemed oblivious to it.

"The bad news gets around in our burg," Isabel said.

"But then so does the good news," Blaine said. "Luckily, we hear more of it than the bad news. What can I do for you?"

"We understand you and Deacon posed with a fish you caught for a newspaper photo," Alma replied.

Grinning as he set aside the push broom, Blaine nodded. "We pulled a whopper of a catfish out of the Cornet River below the railroad bridge. Deacon had the bright idea of having our picture taken with it. I went along with him because I was drooling to chow down as soon as he cooked it over his gas grill."

"Was Laura home to share your feast?" Alma asked.

"We had enough catfish to fill up everybody," Blaine replied. "Laura made the hush puppies, coleslaw, and potato salad. I made the root beer run, and we ate like we were monarchs on their patio. Oh, what a grand evening we had under the stars."

"Do you stay in touch with Deacon?" Alma asked.

"We've remained pals since high school," Blaine replied. "Why?"

"We'd like to talk to him," Alma said. "Where might we find him?"

Blaine shook his head. "He's been coping with Laura's murder while hanging out at their cottage. Give him a day to get over the initial shock."

Isabel traded alarmed glances with Alma.

"He shouldn't be left alone at a traumatic time like now," Isabel said. "Is anybody there with him?"

"If they are, I wasn't told about it," Blaine replied. "I'm shutting the hardware store during my lunch hour and heading over for a visit. He can stand to see a friendly face."

"I should think so." Isabel checked the time on her smartphone. "Lunch is a few hours away, so what's he doing until then?"

"He was playing Solitaire and watching TV when I last phoned him," Blaine replied.

"Is Deacon an impulsive or excitable fellow who might do something regrettably stupid and tragic while he's alone?" Isabel asked.

Alma nodded. "Who knows what you might find when you make it over to his cottage?"

"I take your meaning." Blaine swallowed hard. "It's not a pretty picture you paint, either."

"Murder and its consequences are never pretty," Isabel said.

"I could close up shop now and pay Deacon a visit since I've had no customers this morning," Blaine said.

"If you don't mind, we'd like to tag along with you," Isabel said.

"Are you tagging along as a pair of private eyes?" Blaine asked.

"You may assume we're back on the case," Isabel replied. "Does it cause you any heartburn?"

"As long as you don't make me a murder suspect it doesn't," Blaine replied.

"I think we're safe to say you're not one," Isabel said.

"If we do make you one, we'll let you know," Alma said.

"I'll meet you at his cottage," Blaine said.

The Isherwoods, Deacon and Laura, resided in an eggshell white-shingled cottage with dove gray shutters, a reclaimed slate roof, and a tulip red door. The burgundy and yellow peonies bloomed on each side of the front porch. Blaine had parked in the driveway where he waited for Isabel and Alma, his ankle-high work boot hiked up on the bumper. As they nosed up behind his pickup truck, he spat and gave them a nod.

"The tiny cottage must have the one bedroom, so I guess the Isherwoods had no children," Isabel said.

"Laura never mentioned any children," Alma said. "How shall we approach Deacon?"

"Blaine can break the ice and carry the conversation. If Deacon is in a gregarious mood, we'll ask him a few questions." Isabel drew up the strap to her pocketbook to ride on her forearm. "Shall we hop out and join Blaine?"

"I don't know about you, but I don't hop out of a car anymore," Alma said. "Bending and groaning my way out takes a lot more effort."

The rumpled Deacon with a sunken, sallow face could've used a shave and a haircut. Next to Blaine's beefy physique, Deacon was a rangy man in his mid-thirties with blue eyes set too close together and a prominent, bony nose. His pace was languid as if he never bothered to make haste even if he ran late. Isabel's initial impression of him was an unfavorable one, but her neutral face betrayed nothing she felt.

Blaine and Deacon exchanged hearty greetings and handshakes with Blaine slapping his friend on the shoulder. They'd obviously known each other for a long time. Deacon didn't crack a smile, but his tense face relaxed. He padded barefoot across the parquet floor as he showed them into the tastefully appointed living room Laura had furnished. The faint lemon scent from her furniture polish lingered in the air. Isabel and Alma sat on the beige sofa while Blaine sank into the overstuffed armchair. Deacon returned to the recliner and used the TV remote to switch off the TV. An unfinished hand of Solitaire lay on the card table. Isabel and Alma waited in silence, letting Blaine open the proceedings.

"How are you hitting them, Deacon?" Blaine asked.

"I've had better mornings as recently as yesterday, but I'll keep it together and not go sideways," Deacon replied.

He used a nasally twang Isabel placed as originating from the leafy Blue Ridge Mountains to the west.

"Thanks for coming over," Deacon said. "You didn't have to take off time from work, though."

"Things at the hardware store are slow," Blaine said. "Isabel and Alma came along with me."

"So I noticed," Deacon said. "Are they your kinfolk?"

Blaine laughed a little too brashly. "They wouldn't claim me even if I was related by blood."

"Can you blame them?" Deacon said. "Of course I'm left curious why they accompanied you."

"Because I invited them," Blaine said. "They're friends of mine."

"Uh-huh," Deacon said. "Your friends aren't necessarily my friends, though."

"Is something gnawing at you, Deacon?" Blaine asked.

"I'm just asking the question," Deacon replied, narrow-eyed and sharp-voiced.

"Have you set up Laura's funeral?" Blaine asked.

"I won't be holding a funeral," Deacon replied. "It's too expensive for my bank account, so I'm using the cheaper, easier cremation."

"A cremation serves the same purpose, I reckon," Blaine said. "Where do you plan to scatter her ashes?"

"Say again?" Deacon's face was puzzled.

"Folks customarily scatter the cremated ashes of their loved one at a special place," Blaine replied.

"Laura never had a special place that I know of, so I won't be scattering her ashes anywhere," Deacon said.

"It's your call," Blaine said.

Deacon went on. "I'm stuffing her ashes inside an old one-gallon canning jar and screwing it shut with a lid. She'll rest easy up there on the fireplace mantel with her knickknacks, where all I have to do is blow the dust off her. If I get tired of doing it, I'll bury her ashes down in a peaceful laurel hollow over in the national park."

"The Feds will have a say in it," Blaine said. "Park regulations, you understand."

"The Feds should keep their big nose out of our personal lives," Deacon said.

"Rules are rules we have to follow," Blaine said. "There can be no exceptions, Deacon, even for you."

"Blaine, I need to hear one of your sermons about as much as I need a second navel," Deacon said. "Put a sock in it."

"It's just my friendly advice," Blaine said. "Preachers give sermons, and I sure don't."

"Same difference," Deacon said.

Isabel decided it was an opportune time to break into the men's testy repartee. Her curiosity was killing her, so to speak.

"Did you hear from Laura this morning after she opened up the beauty shop?" Isabel asked.

"Nope," Deacon replied.

They waited quietly, but Deacon added nothing else.

"Did she take her smartphone with her?" Isabel asked.

"Yep," Deacon replied.

"Did she leave for work at her usual time?" Isabel asked.

"Yep," Deacon replied.

"Had she brought up any recent quarrels or reprimands she'd received at the beauty shop?" Isabel asked.

"Nope," Deacon replied.

"Did she like her job cutting hair?" Isabel asked.

"Yep," Deacon replied.

Isabel glanced at Alma. They were going to be here for a while. Alma raised her eyebrows in acknowledgement.

"Did she have any known enemies?" Isabel asked.

"Nope," Deacon replied.

"Did you speak to Farrah about Laura's murder?" Isabel asked.

"Nope," Deacon replied.

"Had Laura acted fearful, anxious, or depressed lately?" Isabel asked.

"Nope," Deacon replied.

Isabel thought using a pair of pliers to pull teeth would be easier than drawing any information out of Deacon. Again, she glanced at Alma who gave a shrug. They'd gotten off to a shaky start. Digging in was their only option, especially after what came next.

Deacon glowered at Blaine. "Why are they sticking their big noses into my personal business as the Feds do?"

Blaine grinned. "Aw shucks, Deacon, they haven't asked you anything I'd consider too personal. Chill out a little."

"I know about them, and what they do at a time like this." Deacon pointed his knobby finger at Isabel and Alma. "I know plenty, all right."

"What do you think you know about us?" Isabel asked.

"You've been written up in the newspaper," Deacon replied. "Do you think folks like me don't read it? You're a pair of meddling busybodies who make a game out of prying into other folks' private affairs."

"Alas, our cover is blown, and you've found us out," Isabel dryly said.

"Isabel and Alma can ferret out who killed Laura faster than you can snap your fingers," Blaine said. "At least I assume you want to know who took her life."

"Her killer should be arrested and punished," Deacon said.

"Why are you so hostile if they're willing to look into it?" Blaine asked.

"Sheriff Fox, not them, is responsible for carrying out justice," Deacon replied.

Blaine grunted. "I can tell you that won't happen anytime soon as long as Sheriff Fox is running the show. If you don't stay on your guard, he'll show up here with a mind to arrest *you*."

"Roscoe and I go back a long way," Deacon said. "He'd never do such a crazy thing to me."

Again, Blaine grunted. "Only a fool wouldn't stay wary of Sheriff Fox. I have personal experience with him targeting me as one of his murder suspects."

"Things must've worked out for you," Deacon said. "You're not stuck behind steel bars clad in an orange jumpsuit and eating a plateful of beans and franks."

"I caught a lucky break is the only reason why I sit here before you," Blaine said.

Isabel decided to ask the rest of her questions before Deacon ordered them to leave. "Did you go to work this morning at your usual time? Please don't be rude. Answer me in complete sentences this time."

"I left here for work at the same time as I always do," Deacon said. "My boss Mr. Dunfee gave me the bad news after he heard it from Sheriff Fox."

"Why didn't he contact you directly?" Isabel asked.

"Because I can't hear my smartphone ringing or vibrating while I'm driving the noisy forklift," Deacon replied.

"Where do you drive the forklift?" Isabel asked.

"I work in the warehouse at the Dunfee Sash and Door Company," Deacon replied.

"Has Sheriff Fox seen you this morning?" Isabel asked.

"Roscoe called me and said he'll be dropping by today," Deacon replied. "I thought you were him parking in the driveway."

"Did Mr. Dunfee send you home?" Isabel asked.

"We get three days of paid bereavement leave, and I didn't want to get cheated out of taking mine," Deacon replied.

"If it were me I'd want to stay busy and keep my mind off the tragedy," Isabel said. "There'll be time to grieve at the funeral with my family and friends grouped around me."

"Then I guess you and I are wired differently," Deacon said.

Isabel smiled primly. "No doubt we are, Mr. Isherwood. Very different, I should think. How did you and Laura first meet?"

However, Deacon was no longer as cooperative. "I know Laura chattered away while she cut hair and filled you in on the details."

"Laura said little if anything about her personal life," Isabel said. "Anytime I asked her, she changed the subject. She didn't tell us Jodie had returned to Quiet Anchorage. I learned to respect Laura's boundaries and her desire for privacy."

"Jodie also has a big nose that she sticks in my personal business," Deacon said.

"You don't think much of your ex-sister-in-law, I take it," Isabel said.

"Quite frankly, I revile and loathe her," Deacon said. "She returns the favor, just the way I want it."

Alma spoke for the first time. "I once asked Laura why she drove a junky car, and she instead told me about the peonies she planted out front. Can you tell me why she drove a car older than ours is?"

"She was a frugal person who was careful about how she spent her money," Deacon replied. "She clipped coupons, scouted for the store sales, and frequented the thrift shops."

"The living room is spotless," Alma said. "I don't see a speck of dust or lint."

"She did the housework," Deacon said. "She was thorough and meticulous in everything she undertook."

"Isn't it ironic how she let her guard down this morning?" Alma said. "You get distracted by something just once, and you pay dearly for it. You're murdered in a beauty shop by a killer who had to know ahead of time when you'd be there." She gave Deacon a direct look.

"Hold on a second," Deacon said. "I had nothing to do with Laura's slaying if that's what you're insinuating."

"Nobody has accused you," Alma said. "We're interested in knowing why Laura was so laconic about her personal life."

"She felt like it was nobody's business, which it isn't," Deacon replied.

"Or maybe she felt ashamed of it," Alma said.

"What is that crack supposed to mean?" Deacon asked.

Alma shrugged with a wry smile. "We're just holding a friendly conversation, Deacon. Hopefully, it means nothing, and we can remain friends."

"Laura and I had a rock-solid marriage founded on our passionate love for each other," Deacon said.

"You don't have to convince us," Alma said. "Sheriff Fox will be a different story when he comes knocking on your door."

"Tell them, Blaine," Deacon said. "You know how it was between Laura and me."

"You seemed like a happy couple," Blaine said. "At least from what I saw of you that was true."

"What you saw is how it was all the time in our marriage," Deacon said.

"Sure thing, Deacon, I have no reason not to believe you," Blaine said. "Except Laura is dead. Somebody killed her. Who did it? Her killer doesn't get a free pass."

Dropping his defiant glower, Deacon gulped. "That's what I'd like to know. All I can say is I wasn't in on it, and I'm an innocent man."

"I have faith the truth will prevail." Blaine glanced at Isabel and Alma. "Are you ready to leave? I have to get back and unpack some new inventory I received this morning."

Isabel nodded. "We'll be leaving. Thanks a mint for indulging us, Deacon."

"Yeah, sure, it was no sweat," Deacon said. "Come back anytime you like. Sorry if I was a little short-tempered with you. I'm not myself today."

"You're having one bad day is all," Isabel said. "Tomorrow will be better."

Alma nodded at the card table displaying the in-progress game of Solitaire. "You can play the queen of hearts on the king of hearts."

Deacon studied the playing cards. "Yeah, so, I can. Good catch, Alma. Thanks."

Deacon said nothing else as they left. He'd make out fine while he was left alone at the cottage. This time Alma crawled behind the steering wheel since the sisters took turns with the driving duties. Blaine sped off back to town in his car. Mulling over their encounter with Deacon, Isabel gazed out the car window. She noticed the roadside stalks of chicory blooming with its delicate blue and purple flowers. The elegant Queen Anne's lace was also flowering. She expected to notice the crook-shaped goldenrod turning brassy yellow before long.

"Deacon didn't give a good accounting of himself," Alma said.

"He has a funny way of expressing his grief," Isabel said. "I'm not ready to say he killed Laura, but he doesn't like us looking into it."

Alma nodded. "Deacon might be hiding something. Maybe his marriage wasn't the rock-solid one he purports it was. We came this morning in search of a motive for Laura's murder, and we may have well found it."

"I agree. Will Sheriff Fox see it the same way after he speaks to Deacon?"

"We can't depend on Sheriff Fox for closely questioning Deacon since they're good ole boys and friends."

"For better or worse, Sheriff Fox depends on us to do the brunt of the homicide investigating."

Alma had a mirthless laugh. "He's taking advantage of our willingness to snoop while he sits back twiddling his thumbs." Isabel nodded. "Just between you and me, he's turned into one of the laziest men God ever put breath in."

"Amen to that sentiment, sister," Alma said.

Chapter 3

Sammi Jo Garner, a sturdy, striking twentysomething with wheat blonde hair she wore short, was on the verge of flinging an old-fashioned hissy fit. A close friend of the Trumbo sisters, she'd sleuthed alongside them since their first murder mystery (a total of eleven cases to date). Sitting in their armchairs, they were doing their best to calm her down while she paced the living room. She was having more boyfriend issues that never seemed any closer to a resolution.

"Reynolds Kyle has shown me his true ornery self," Sammi Jo said, her tone angry. "I'm glad I found out who he is before we tied the knot."

"So am I," Alma said. "Isabel and I would need a miracle to bail you out of prison after you shot down Reynolds in his tracks."

Isabel frowned with her disapproval at Alma.

"Shooting would be too good for him," Sammi Jo said. "I'd feed him, piece by piece, to the hungry sharks."

"Where did you say Reynolds went?" Isabel asked.

"He and his rat pack lit out for the Darlington Raceway in South Carolina," Sammi Jo replied. "Once he was on the road, he sent me a text. A text! Can you believe the unmitigated gall? He doesn't have the guts to tell me to my face he's skipped town. He promised we'd talk about setting our wedding date."

"The race car fever burns in the young man's blood," Alma said.

Again, Isabel frowned at Alma.

"I don't give two hoots and a holler about his blood ailment," Sammi Jo said. "He made a commitment, and he should keep it."

"Maybe now is the right time to cut your losses and be done with Reynolds," Alma said. "Since all Isabel can do is frown, I'll give you our frank counsel. We see lots of other single young guys who are handsome and employed."

"I'd follow your frank counsel except for one small matter," Sammi Jo said.

"You still love your guy," Isabel said, her voice clear and steady.

"Bingo. Is there any known cure for it?" Sammi Jo asked. "Does Eustis stock any pills, nostrums, or potions at the pharmacy?"

"It doesn't hurt to ask him, but I'd say no," Isabel replied. "Reynolds is too easily distracted and has the attention span of a goldfish."

"Tell me about it," Sammi Jo said.

"Look, just text Reynolds back and say you want to set a firm wedding date when he returns home," Alma said. "You don't want to hear any ifs, ands, or buts about it."

"I guess I can give it a try," Sammi Jo said.

"Nothing ventured, nothing gained," Alma said.

"There, we've put it to bed," Isabel said with a relieved smile. "The other important topic is murder."

"First, we eat lunch at Eddy's Deli, and then we can work on the murder case," Alma said, standing up.

"Goodness me, I've been so caught up in Sammi Jo's romance woes that I forgot about our lunch," Isabel said.

"Rest assured anytime you do, I'll be certain to remind you," Alma said.

"I don't know how to break the bad news, so I'll just say it," Sammi Jo said. "Eddy's Deli is closed."

Alma froze in stunned silence for a moment before she recovered. "Is Eddy's Deli permanently shut?"

"Eddy is having some electrical wiring done in the kitchen that will take a few hours to complete," Sammi Jo replied.

"We'll have to drive all the way to Warrenton for lunch," Alma said. "I'll die of starvation before we get there."

"You're far from that happening," Isabel told her roly-poly sister.

"I have a backup plan in mind if you'd like to hear it," Sammi Jo said.

"What is it?" Isabel asked.

"We'll sit down at the drugstore's soda fountain and order banana splits," Sammi Jo replied. "They're not high in nutrition, but we need the extra calories while we're under the additional strain of pursuing a killer."

"Plus, the banana splits taste so irresistibly delicious," Isabel said.

Since the day was a sunny one, they walked from the sisters' house on Church Street to the town drugstore on Main Street. Isabel brought Petey Samson on his leash because he needed the exercise before he went stir crazy, or he drove them crazy. As beagles do, his keen nose picked up the alluring scents he yearned to sprint off and explore more fully.

He strained on the leash, and Isabel clutched it tighter. She snapped her fingers, and he knew he'd better stop his rambunctious behavior, or he'd receive no doggie treats. He lived for wolfing them down.

While not an old fogey stuck in the past, Isabel took immense pleasure in entering the quaint town drugstore. The first aromas greeting her were the cherry-flavored cough drops and the sweet smell of gumballs. The gnarly pine floor planks reminded her of the farmhouse where she'd grown up. She admired the apothecary display cabinets constructed of brownish oak with the locking glass doors. They sat on the red vinyl swivel stools lining the soda fountain, a steel and pink marble beauty. Petey Samson curled up on the floor, yawned, and dozed off.

"Remind me to pick up cocoa butter and witch hazel," Alma said.

"I will if you remember I need lip balm and cold cream," Isabel said.

"I'll probably think of something else, too," Alma said.

Isabel did a visual sweep. "Is Eustis holed up in the backroom counting his pills?"

"He counts them to keep us in good health," Sammi Jo replied.

"Even a diligent pill counter needs to take a break," Isabel said.

"Where is my banana split?" Alma asked.

"I can hop behind the counter and fix them," Sammi Jo replied. "I've never done it before, but it's not making a lunar landing."

"Are the bananas green?" Alma asked. "Mine have to be ripe enough to attract fruit flies."

"Alma, no fruit flies are in the drugstore," Isabel said.

"How do you know?" Alma asked. "Are you suddenly the world's Ph.D. authority on the fruit fly?"

"I might know a fact or two about the fruit fly," Isabel replied.

"Oh yeah? Then name one fruit fly fact I don't already know," Alma said.

"Did you know fruit flies in some cultures are considered a delicacy?" Isabel said.

Before Alma could respond, Eustis hustled up, smiling and waving. He wasn't a true native of Quiet Anchorage--known locally as a townie--but everybody liked him just the same. A gangly man endowed with more brains than brawn, he'd gone bald as a peeled onion. His pharmacist coat, bow tie, and pleated trousers lent him a studious bent. Sammi Jo affectionately called him a nerd, and he didn't mind. Anything she said was swell since he'd had a longtime crush on her.

"Have you heard the big news?" Eustis lumbered behind the soda fountain. "Murder has rocked our town! Again!" He paused to rein in his inappropriate excitement. "That is to say a murderer is on the rampage who must be quickly and efficiently apprehended to make our town streets safe."

"We got word about Laura Isherwood's murder," Isabel replied.

"Not only that, but Sheriff Fox asked us for a hand, so how could we refuse him?" Alma said.

"You wouldn't dream of it," Eustis said. "He needs his brilliant sleuths toiling in close concert with him. That's how we do things in Quiet Anchorage. What's your order, ladies?"

"We'll each have a banana split," Alma replied.

Eustis washed his hands and peeled the bananas. "Did you know Laura?"

"She was our hairstylist who gave us the coif we had in mind," Alma replied. "If I brought a picture of a movie star's hairstyle I liked, she nailed it right."

"We're devastated over what happened to her," Isabel said.

"You have no choice but to track down her killer," Eustis said. "Will you need a sidekick?"

"Well, you see--," Isabel said.

"As you know, I'm well prepared," Eustis said. "My blue plaid fedora and trench coat hang on the wall pegs in my office. I bought a zoom lens camera and night vision goggles to use while I'm on my first stakeout."

"If we require the services of a hardboiled private eye, we know who to see first," Isabel said.

"I'm available 24x7," Eustis said. "Have you developed any murder suspects?"

"We can't divulge how our murder case is proceeding," Alma replied. "It remains hush-hush, you understand."

Sammi Jo rolled her eyes at Eustis.

"We just began looking into it." Isabel waved her hand at Eustis. "Don't sprinkle any crushed walnuts and pineapple on my banana split. I'm watching my girlish figure in case my Hollywood agent calls."

"Sprinkle Isabel's crushed walnuts and pineapple on my banana split," Alma said. "There's no sense in letting them go to waste."

"I've got you covered," Eustis said. "Would you like any chocolate syrup, Isabel?"

"Just dribble her chocolate syrup all over mine," Alma said.

"Thanks just the same, but I'll eat my chocolate syrup," Isabel said.

"I thought you just said you're a skinny Minnie," Alma said.

"I'm counting my calories, not depriving myself of everything fun," Isabel said.

"Was Laura one of your customers?" Sammi Jo asked.

Eustis set the three long glass dishes holding the banana splits on the counter with the spoons and napkins. Alma beat Isabel and Sammi Jo at diving into hers.

"Not long ago Laura came in with her older sister Jodie Wright," Eustis replied. "Have you met Jodie? She took the bookkeeper's position at the Blevins Millworks."

Isabel furrowed her forehead in surprise. "Laura never mentioned it. Alma, did you hear Laura say anything about Jodie's return?"

Alma shook her head. The banana split filled her bulging cheeks like a chipmunk, and she couldn't speak clearly.

"What's Jodie's story?" Sammi Jo asked.

"I heard she moved back here from Richmond," Eustis replied.

"Is she another country gal who had her fill of city life and grew homesick for her small-town roots?" Sammi Jo asked.

"She finalized her divorce and relocated to get away from her ex," Eustis replied.

"That'd be enough incentive for me to hotfoot it out of Richmond," Alma said. "I wouldn't live in the same hemisphere with either of my exes."

"Your exes still live in Virginia as far as we know," Isabel said.

"Obviously, I'm using hyperbole to amplify my point," Alma said.

"Did you speak to Jodie and Laura?" Isabel asked.

"They murmured and never made eye contact with me until they brought their purchases to the checkout counter," Eustis replied. "Laura introduced me to Jodie after I asked if she was Laura's sister. They were the spitting images of each other, and Laura didn't seem too happy. She growled and never smiled."

"Maybe they'd been quarreling," Alma said. "Sisters grate on each other's nerves and act grouchy, but they clear the air, and things go back to normal. Isn't it true, Isabel?"

"Sisters should look out for each other and remain friends for life," Isabel replied. "However, it takes a herculean effort, especially if the younger sister is oftentimes a nincompoop."

"Isabel and Alma, now isn't the time to resurrect your old nincompoop's spat," Eustis said. "Too much detective work needs your attention."

"We nincompoops are also first-rate snoops," Alma said.

"Nincompoops can also pick up the tab," Isabel said. "Pay Eustis for our banana splits. Meantime, I have to take Petey Samson out to stretch his legs."

"The darling is also overdue for his next doggie treat." Alma took one from her pocketbook, and he gobbled it down.

"You and Isabel dote on your pet more than any of my other customers do with theirs," Eustis said.

"Petey Samson is more than our pet," Alma said. "He's a beloved member of the family. Isn't he, Isabel?"

"You bet your sweet bippy he is," Isabel replied.

"Can we say, then, he's your fur baby?" Eustis asked.

"Of course we can," Alma replied. "Isn't he, Isabel?"

"Well, let's not get too carried away with our rosy sentiments," Isabel replied.

Chapter 4

Blevins Millworks, a family-owned lumberyard, operated on the far side of the railroad tracks. Archie Blevins did more than sell lumber. He also built modular homes and booked side construction projects like in-law suites, porches, and sundecks. With the influx of new residents moving into the subdivisions springing up, Archie did quite well for himself and his family. He drove a flashy Audi, vacationed in Acapulco, and resided in a new Victorian Revival spacious enough to hold a town hall meeting.

With all the jobs Archie was getting and his profits surging, he needed an experienced bookkeeper. He had a knack for hustling up new work and making persuasive sales pitches, but he disliked anything to do with office management, which he avoided like he did building inspectors. So, he hired Jodie Wright to handle the administrative side.

At present, Petey Samson, tugging on his leash and panting, led Isabel, Alma, and Sammi Jo down the sidewalk. They approached the town bank, a two-story brick building topped with a white cupola and a black rooster weathervane. As they passed the entrance to the bank's parking lot, Isabel noticed a young lady closing her car door. When she turned around and looked ahead, the sunlight spilled across her face.

She bore a striking resemblance to Laura Isherwood. *Jodie Wright*, Isabel recognized as her pulse ticked up a notch. They wouldn't have to find Jodie because she'd found them even if she didn't realize it yet. Alma had the same reaction.

"Talk about your serendipity in play," Alma said. "Will Jodie talk to us about Laura?"

"The chances are promising if we put her on the spot," Isabel replied.

With the strap to a bulky purse slung over her shoulder, Jodie strolled toward the bank's entrance. She was taller and heavier than Laura. Jodie's red lipstick, side-swept bob, and dress suit made her look slim, confident, and smart. Drawing close enough to flash her blue eyes at them, she had a tentative smile as she sought to place who they were. However, she didn't recognize them.

"Are you, by any chance, Laura Isherwood's sister?" Alma asked.

Stopping three paces away, Jodie nodded. "Yes, I'm Jodie Wright, and Laura was my younger sister," she replied in a well-modulated voice.

"Didn't you return after your divorce in Richmond?" Alma asked.

"I haven't made it a secret I divorced Bernie Wright," Jodie replied. "What's it to you anyway?"

Alma made the quick introductions, and Jodie barely glanced at Isabel and Sammi Jo. Shifting the strap to her bulky purse, she knitted her eyebrows together.

"A creep murdered Laura this morning," Jodie said.

"Being sisters, we know how close they can be," Alma said.

"Indeed so," Isabel said.

"How did you know Laura?" Relaxing a little, Jodie was less guarded. "I don't remember any of your faces or names."

"Laura was our longtime hairstylist," Alma replied.

"You lost your hairstylist while I lost my sister," Jodie said. "We have, I suppose, something in common."

Alma glanced at Isabel.

"We're sorry for your loss," Isabel said. "We'd grown quite fond of Laura. Everybody we know is taking her death very hard. She will be missed by many of us."

"Your condolences are appreciated," Jodie said. "It's comforting to learn how many customers and friends she had in Quiet Anchorage."

"We've taken an active role in her murder." Isabel laughed. "You could say we're part of her murder investigation."

"Now I'm confused," Jodie said.

"Well, you see, it's like this," Isabel said. "We're a little different than the other townies."

"You don't look any different to me," Jodie said.

"We're honest-to-goodness amateur sleuths," Isabel replied. "You've probably watched the inquisitive women like us doing their sleuthing on TV or maybe in the movies. I can understand if you have doubts. However, I assure you we're not crackpots, and we have an established track record of success."

"What is this anyway? Are you yanking my chain?" Jodie asked.

"If you don't believe us, ask Rosie and Lotus at Clean Vito's," Isabel replied. "Or you can check with the Three Musketeers sitting on the wooden bench. Just about any townie will vouch for our claim."

"For the sake of expediency, I'll play along with you," Jodie said. "Are you sleuthing--such an odd term--on Laura's murder case?"

Isabel smiled. "You've got it. May we ask you our questions?"

"Okay, but make it a couple," Jodie replied. "I have to return to the office."

"When did you last see or speak to Laura?" Isabel asked.

"Last week--was it on Tuesday afternoon?--Laura and I blocked out some free time to go clothes shopping at the mall," Jodie replied.

"Was Laura her usual self?" Isabel asked. "Did you pick up on anything different about her?"

"She was plain old Laura," Jodie replied. "We had a pleasant outing, bought several small articles on sale, and I treated us to dinner at a seafood house. She dined on crab cakes, and I had the lobster bisque. We looked forward to our next outing together."

"Did you schedule the day and time of your next outing?" Isabel asked.

"Nothing was settled," Jodie replied.

"Did she mention anything wrong at the beauty shop or in her marriage?" Isabel asked.

"She said nothing like that," Jodie replied. "Look, I don't mean to break this up, but Archie will be irate if I spend too much time away. I'm skipping lunch, and I'll probably be staying late again. I'm not complaining, mind you, but I fear I'm becoming a workaholic."

"Is your bank trip for business or personal reasons?" Isabel asked.

"I make my bank trip daily," Jodie replied. "Archie prefers for our customers to pay us in cash, and he doesn't want it lying around. The word spreads, and the wrong person hears it. Who wants to stare down the business end of a Saturday Night Special?"

"I wouldn't fret over a robbery," Alma said. "Quiet Anchorage has far more homicides than it does thefts."

"Alma!" Isabel said, taken aback. "Please."

"What did I say now?" Alma asked, blinking at Isabel.

"Try to exercise a little tact and restraint," Isabel replied. "I swear you'll blurt out anything that bubbles up in your head."

Alma shrugged. "Nobody in Quiet Anchorage is more appalled by it than me. But it is what it is, so why should we sugarcoat it?"

"If I'd known of your murder trend, I would've remained living in Richmond," Jodie said.

"Most of the townies are law-abiding, peace-loving citizens," Isabel said. "From time to time, a murder crops up and disturbs the peace. Surely, you heard about it while you were away. Laura must have brought it up with you."

Jodie pivoted toward the bank entrance. "If she did, I have no recollection of it. Quiet Anchorage has become like a city, and the bucolic small town I knew as a girl in is no more. Sad, isn't it? I hope the sheriff is busy closing out Laura's murder, so I can get some sleep again."

"Busy is debatable," Alma said. "Sheriff Fox likes to take his sweet time while doing things his way."

"So I heard, but I was giving him the benefit of the doubt," Jodie said. "I'd hate for it to drag on unresolved for months."

"Has he taken down your written statement?" Isabel asked.

"He didn't question me," Jodie replied. "Who was the deputy sheriff stopping by? I can picture his chubby, freckled face, but his name eludes me."

"Was he a doofus?" Alma asked.

"Doofus?" Jodie said. "Define a doofus for me."

"Was he clearing his throat, gnawing on his pencil stub, and hungrily sizing up your lunch?" Alma asked.

"You describe him to a T," Jodie replied.

"Then he's got to be Deputy Sheriff Bexley," Alma said.

"Yes, Bexley is the name he gave me," Jodie said.

Isabel, Alma, and Sammi Jo let out a collective sigh. Even Petey Samson seemed to roll his soulful brown eyes and shake his head at hearing the news.

"Is something wrong?" Jodie asked.

"We'll just say Deputy Sheriff Bexley does his level best at discharging his law enforcement duties," Isabel said.

"I gave him everything I know on Laura," Jodie said. "I don't have a lot. We didn't stay in touch as much while I was away living in Richmond, and we were still catching up on old times."

"How involved were you in each other's lives?" Isabel asked.

"We chatted almost daily and sometimes more often," Jodie replied. "I loved my sister, and we took up right where we'd left off." Her eyes welled up in tears as she opened her bulky purse to get something. "Lord knows I'll miss the squirt. We'll take no more shopping trips together. She was the only family I had living in the area." She blotted a folded tissue under each eye to absorb the tears. "Look at silly me. I'll ruin my mascara and look a frightful mess."

"Do you have an opinion of her husband Deacon?" Isabel asked.

Jodie used a vulgar word leaving no room for doubt she had low regard for him. Isabel could sympathize. He'd exhibited a sullen indifference to them over the loss of his murdered wife. On the other hand, she wanted to maintain an open mind and not rush to judgment at this early stage.

"Have you any inkling of who'd want to kill Laura?" Isabel asked.

"As I told Deputy Sheriff Bexley, any name I give would be just a wild guess," Jodie replied.

"Fair enough," Isabel said. "We've reached a good stopping point."

Jodie hoisted her bulky purse. "I should make this bank deposit and return to the office."

"Thanks for taking our questions," Isabel said.

"It wasn't an imposition," Jodie said. "Let's hope our next meeting will be more convivial and pleasant."

"We'll hope for the same thing," Isabel said. "You take care now."

Isabel waited until Jodie had left them and disappeared into the bank lobby. "I'd be willing to wager my next glass of iced tea our second murder suspect just left us and sauntered into the bank."

"You sure got that part right," Alma said.

"I'll chime in and add my vote," Sammi Jo said.

"Then it's passed by unanimous decree," Isabel said.

"What next step makes the most sense to take?" Alma asked.

"The Three Musketeers usually have something worthwhile to share with us," Isabel replied.

"We haven't seen them in quite a while," Alma said.

"Shall I tell them we're coming?" Sammi Jo asked, smartphone in hand.

"Please do rouse them," Isabel replied. "They should be awake from their catnaps by the time we arrive."

"I sure wouldn't bet my next glass of iced tea on it," Alma said.

Petey Samson led them away from the bank, his beagle nose sniffing the ground. He reminded Isabel of themselves so diligently searching hither and yon for the clues. He viewed it as a big adventure while they did much the same thing.

Chapter 5

Every small town worth its ink dot on the map has its cast of colorful characters and eccentrics, and Quiet Anchorage's trio perched on the wooden bench--also known as the liars' bench--by the entrance to the Azul Lagos Florist Shop. Corina Moccasin owned it, and she barely tolerated the Three Musketeers led by her favorite uncle, Willie Moccasin. His cohorts Blue Trent and Ossie Conger sat next to Willie. More often than not, they were the only thing on Main Street registering a pulse, particularly on a summer weekday afternoon.

They dressed alike in Madras shorts, tie-dye t-shirts, and Teva sandals. The dog tags dangling on the bead chains around their necks were the real deal from their World War Two military service. They carried their smartphones on lanyards. On occasion, they sported summery fedoras. Well along into their eighties, they often acted as if they were mischievous teenage boys again who'd do or say just about anything for a laugh.

"Blue, I checked my desk calendar before I left the house, and today is your turn to gripe," Willie said. "So then, tell us how you're making out with your scaly skin rash."

"I'm pleased as punch to report it's vanished." With a broad grin, Blue did a double thumbs up. "The doc's stinky orange salve I rubbed on it worked a miracle cure." He reared upright, reached down to unhitch his belt buckle, and pivoted to bend over in front of them. "You should see it for yourselves. It'll blow your minds--totally."

"Um, just keep your pants on, Blue," Willie said, hands up and recoiling in horror.

"No, I mean it, guys. Seeing is believing," Blue said. "Did either of you bring a selfie stick? I'd love to take a snapshot for posterity."

"Ossie and I will take your word for it," Willie said. "No show and tell is necessary."

Ossie rubbed his eyes. "Blech! I didn't need to see that mental picture. Blech! Thanks for ruining my day, Blue." Again, he rubbed his eyes. "Blech!"

"Suit yourselves." Blue took his seat on the wooden bench. "It's your big loss and not mine."

"Moving right along, we'll take up any new deaths occurring since we last convened," Willie said.

"Nobody has kicked the bucket in days, weeks even," Ossie said.

"Well, has Sheriff Fox or Deputy Sheriff Bexley arrested any scofflaw for littering, jaywalking, or loitering?" Willie asked.

"Again, we got nothing," Ossie replied. "Life has turned excruciatingly humdrum and dull around here."

"Surely, there's something--anything!--for us to discuss," Willie said. "Who's cheating on whom? Who was chased off Lovers' Lane? Have you heard any juicy rumors of a tryst at the no-tell motel or seedy bed and breakfast?"

"Nary a one, I'm afraid," Ossie replied. "Everybody has been on their good behavior despite the summer swelter that usually triggers an itch somebody can't resist scratching."

"Hearing all this dismal news puts me in a funk," Blue said. "Quiet Anchorage has let us down."

"Take heart and give it a little more time," Willie said. "I know carnal human nature, and you can bet your next Social Security check some townie will soon do something scandalous. It's in the cards."

Ossie rubbed his hands together as if in wicked glee. "I can't wait until they do and spice up things."

"Meantime, we'll sit here on the wooden bench like three clams at high tide," Blue said.

"Even the clams at high tide need a way to while away their time," Willie said.

"I can show you my--," Blue said, reaching down for his belt buckle.

"No way!" Willie said.

"Did either of you bring dice for shooting craps?" Ossie asked.

"We can't anymore," Blue replied.

"Why is that?" Ossie asked.

"Corina outlawed any gambling," Willie replied.

"Did you tell her we're just betting toothpicks or jelly beans?" Ossie said.

"It makes no difference," Willie said. "Corina says gambling is gambling."

"Corina is too uptight," Blue said. "She needs to practice yoga or see a therapist. Or better yet, she needs to get some good loving."

"Don't we all, Blue," Ossie said. "Don't we all."

"Speak for yourselves," Willie said, his expression smug and superior.

"How can you have some action going on at your ripe old age?" Ossie asked.

"I pop the little blue pill," Willie replied.

"Huh?" Ossie gawked at Willie. "What little blue pill is that?"

Blue suppressed his fit of giggles.

"Do you live under a rock?" Willie said.

"Maybe I don't get out much," Ossie replied. "Give me the inside skinny."

"It stirs up your sap," Willie said. "You'll feel like a gray stallion."

"With your creaky old ticker, you're kidding me," Ossie said.

"I kid you not," Willie said. "May God strike me dead if I am."

"My sap hasn't been stirred up since leisure suits went out of fashion," Ossie said.

"You don't know what you're missing," Willie said. "Go see your doctor."

"I appreciate the tip," Ossie said. "I'll make an appointment today."

"Your stirred-up sap will thank you in spades," Willie said.

"Ain't modern medicine the bomb?" Blue said.

"It's all that plus a bag of chips," Willie said.

"Tell us about your latest UFO sightings," Ossie said.

Chin dropping, Willie looked forlorn. "I haven't spotted one UFO hovering in the night sky since last week. They've stopped making their flyovers of our town. We don't rate anymore in their celestial flight plans."

"They'll return before you know it," Ossie said while patting Willie on the shoulder. "There's no place in the world quite like Quiet Anchorage."

A croaky noise sounded from somewhere on the wooden bench.

Ossie gazed around. "Did one of you belch or step on a frog?"

"You heard my new ringtone," Willie replied, checking his smartphone. "Sammi Jo sent me a text. She says they're on their way over to see us."

"I hope they bring us some exciting news," Willie said.

"Your wish is her command," Ossie said. "Sammi Jo says they're working on a new murder case."

"What? Murder? Here?" The visibly perturbed Blue sat bolt upright. "A lurid murder has been committed practically under our noses, and we're only learning of it now in Sammi Jo's text. How can that be? Have we lost our keen edge? Are we slipping in our vigilance?"

"I urge launching an immediate investigation to determine how we missed it," Willie replied.

"We've been taking too many catnaps," Ossie said. "I vow to decrease the number and remain more watchful."

"I second it," Blue said. "I can sleep when I'm buried six feet under at my final rest."

"Here's what we'll do when the ladies arrive," Willie said. "We'll pretend as if we knew about the murder and tell them we've been looking into it."

"Bah, you'll never fool them," Ossie said. "You're the lousiest excuse for a liar next to Blue and me."

"Zip it, guys," Willie said. "Here they come. Stay alert and act halfway intelligent. Hear me, Blue?"

"You tend to your business and let me do the same with mine, and we'll be in fine shape," Blue replied.

Isabel hailed the Three Musketeers. "What's been happening with you three gentlemen?"

"We've been discussing the new murder case," Willie replied. "We're as eager as anybody is to know who killed him."

"That's marvelous, Willie, except for one thing," Sammi Jo said. "The murder victim is *her*, not him."

"My bad then," Willie said. "Who was she?"

"Laura Isherwood was a lovely lady and a dear friend," Isabel replied.

"What do you know about Laura?" Willie asked.

"Laura was a master hairstylist employed at Farrah's Beauty Shop," Ossie replied. "She took her time and was aces at cutting hair. Her customers raving over her talent gave her generous tips." Ossie realized his gaffe and quickly added, "Or so I've heard from the different women."

"Naw, that's not how you know so much about Laura," Blue said.

"What do you mean?" Ossie asked.

"Marvin and I chatted," Blue replied. "He said you haven't been to his barbershop all summer."

Willie squinted at Ossie. "Has your hair stopped growing? Are you wearing a skull rug? Or is that a gerbil squatting on your head?"

"Okay, so I patronized Farrah's Beauty Shop, and Laura styled my hair," Ossie said. "She gave a better trim than Marvin does."

"What's wrong with Marvin?" Willie asked.

"He talks and snips, talks and snips while I squirm in the barber chair," Ossie replied. "I could shriek like a lunatic and yank out the rest of my hair. He douses my scalp with a skunky hair tonic. I go home and have to shampoo twice to scrub it out. Where does he buy the gunk?"

"You're probably better off not knowing," Blue replied.

"You're like us in search of a new hairstylist," Alma said.

"Keep me informed of your progress, and I'll reciprocate," Ossie said.

"You've got a deal," Alma said.

"We're discussing a town murder, not tracking down a new hairstylist," Isabel said. "Laura was bumped off in the beauty shop before the other hairstylists arrived."

"Was her killer lying in wait for her?" Willie asked.

"No, Willie. Her killer materialized in a sparkly puff of pixie dust like a magic genie," Ossie replied. "Of course Laura was dry-gulched."

"Well, thanks for clearing that up for me, Tex," Willie said.

"Have you zeroed in on any murder suspects?" Ossie asked.

"We have found two suspects so far," Isabel replied.

"Who are they?" Ossie asked.

"She's not going to tell you who they are," Willie replied. "We know what a blabbermouth you are."

Blue snickered.

"Pipe down and let her speak her piece," Ossie said. "Go ahead, Isabel."

"We're not revealing the murder suspects' names just yet," Isabel said.

Willie stuck out his tongue at Ossie. "You see? I told you so."

"We accepted the murder case a few hours ago, and we're still getting our legs under us," Isabel said.

"If I had to name names, I'd say your two murder suspects are Farrah and Willie," Ossie said.

"How did I wind up on your list?" Willie asked.

"You needled me for having Laura cut my hair," Ossie replied. "Paybacks hurt. I'll visit you while you're doing hard time in the state pen."

"We can eliminate Willie as a murder suspect," Isabel said. "But I'm interested to know why you selected Farrah."

"Farrah was Laura's boss," Ossie replied. "She was in a position of authority over Laura and the logical choice for me to make."

"We'll keep Ossie's thought in mind while we're talking to Farrah," Isabel said.

"Make her and everybody else, too, answer your questions," Ossie said.

"They already know to do that, Ossie," Willie said. "You don't have to tell them."

"My reminding them underscores its importance," Ossie said.

"None of us will rest easy until we chase down all the leads," Isabel said. "Is there anything else we should know about?"

"Just that I'm proud as a peacock to report my scaly skin rash has cleared up," Blue replied, arising from the wooden bench. "Would you like to take a gander at it?" He turned around.

"Thank you, but that's quite all right, Blue," Isabel replied.

"It won't take me but a few moments," Blue said.

"We'll just be happy for you," Isabel said.

"Why does everybody keep telling me that?" Blue said, sitting back down on the wooden bench.

ℌ ℌ ℌ

"What a brazen hussy that Chastity is!" Shaking her fist, Alma hissed and booed at the TV program. "But she didn't fool me for one second. I saw her diabolical nature at work under her smooth façade. This ain't Alma Trumbo's first rodeo."

Isabel also sitting in her armchair looked up from the mystery open on her lap. "How is the episode of your soap opera?"

"It reeks of deceit, jealousy, and betrayal--just the nasty way I like them."

"Is it any different than real life is in Quiet Anchorage?"

"How's that?"

"Deceit, jealousy, and betrayal are the prime motives for murder."

"Huh?"

"Take Laura's murder, for instance. Jealousy may have driven any of the three suspects Deacon Isherwood, Jodie Wright, or Farrah Patel to take her life. However, we need to gather more background information. Alma, have you listened to a single word I said?"

"*Sh-h-h*, Isabel." Alma put her finger to her lips and signaled for quiet. "The climax is coming up, and I want to hear if I'm right about whose baby it is."

Isabel quirked her lips in annoyance, then said, "I wish you'd unleash some of your brainpower on figuring out who killed Laura."

"Yes! I knew it! Cassius is the father!" Alma did a fist pump. "Men are pigs, I swear."

"Just a rotten few of them are, Alma."

"I'm engrossed in watching my soap opera. We'll have to take it up later."

"I don't mind waiting for your soap opera to end. Meantime, I'll continue reading my mystery."

"Whatever suits you is fine by me," Alma said.

Just then, the TV screen clicked and went blank.

"Hey! What just happened?" Alma hopped up and pounded her fist on the TV set. "Is the cable out again? Did a backhoe operator digging outdoors cut the fiber optic cable?"

"The electric power must've cut off since my table lamp also died."

"But it can't blackout in the middle of my soap opera. Get the power company on the line and report our outage."

"Breathe again and relax. It usually flickers back on in an hour or so."

"I can't wait for an hour! Let's buckle up, hurry down to Eddy's Deli, and I'll watch the rest of it on his TV."

Isabel laughed. "Don't be so flighty and settle down."

"That's easy for you to say, but I'm addicted to the soap operas."

"You make it sound dire. Is there such a therapy as Soap Operas Anonymous?"

"Medicare wouldn't cover it even if there was."

Isabel sighed as she picked up her pocketbook. "All right, we'll go on to Eddy's Deli."

"Chastity and Cassius will get married." Alma also grabbed her pocketbook. "They're two nasty peas in a pod who were made for each other."

"She's the town hussy, you know."

"You said a mouthful. Is Sammi Jo free?"

"I think she's catching up on doing her laundry and grocery shopping."

"Don't forget we have a new murder case to continue wrestling with in our spare time."

"What do you think I've been trying to talk to you about for the past hour?"

"Were you? I guess my soap opera distracted me. Well, my old brain is fried. We'll sleep on it and start fresh tomorrow morning."

"We're not making a lot of headway," Isabel said. "I'm getting a little concerned, too. I'm of the mind our sleuthing came easier on our earlier murder mysteries, and we solved them faster."

"You know what? You think too much," Alma said.

Chapter 6

The next morning at the brick rambler, Isabel awoke to Mr. Mockingbird. Perched on a willow tree branch, he was singing his heart out mere inches from her open bedroom window. She'd read where killing a mockingbird was a sin, but this garrulous one disrupting her sleep tested the limits of her tolerance. Then just as swiftly, her crabby mood passed, and she was fine.

Isabel thought of hopping up and fixing breakfast before she dismissed the idea as too ambitious. Besides, Alma was the better cook. Isabel sat up, leaned back against the pillow, and flipped on the headboard lamp. Yawning, she stretched her arms overhead before she cracked her knuckles and rubbed her eyes, preparations for diving into her next reading session.

After turning on to her right side, Isabel surveyed the leaning column of paperbacks--"Mount To-Be-Read"--she'd stacked on the night table. She'd left a bookmark in each paperback since she liked to read several--actually, it was up to a half-dozen paperbacks now-- at the same time. The unorthodox practice made Alma batty.

Isabel deliberated over if she was in the right mood to enter the fictional world of Agatha Christie, Margaret Millar, or Dorothy Uhnak. The lady authors were deceased, but their stirring words lived on in their classic mysteries. Isabel would've jumped at the invitation to attend a coffee klatch with any of them. She might even bring Alma if she hadn't been too much of a nincompoop that week. As Isabel selected the Dorothy Uhnak paperback from the stack without it tumbling over, her smartphone rang. Chuckling, Isabel accepted the call.

"Hello, Alma. You rang me early this morning."

"How could I get any shuteye when Mr. Mockingbird struck up his lively medley? He has the entire town to find a perch and sing, but he decides to alight just outside my open bedroom window, bless his little heart."

"His jaunty song also jarred me awake. However, I like hearing him now."

"Are you cooking breakfast? I have a few items in mind. Have you got a pencil and paper?"

"We'll get dressed, and Eddy can serve us breakfast. How does ordering his blue-plate special sound? Today's is scrambled eggs, grits, smoked bacon, blueberry muffins, fresh strawberries, and all the hot, black coffee you can drink."

"I could go for that in a big way."

"Mrs. Clatterbuck said Eddy may close his diner on Mondays."

"Perish the thought!"

"Lots of the other delis and cafés do."

"I rue the Monday it ever comes to pass." Alma sighed. "Okay, you also had a chance to sleep on the new murder case. Do you have any fresh insights to share?"

"We should never discuss a murder case until after breakfast."

Alma ignored Isabel's silliness. "We have a full day ahead of us."

"What do you say we get with Laura's employer Farrah first?"

"I'll give her a call and see if she has a free moment. She's a dog lover, so we'll bring Petey Samson to give us something else to talk about."

"Every dog lover adores Petey Samson. How could they not? Isn't he the most adorable pooch you've ever laid eyes on?"

"Well, Sheriff Fox thinks otherwise," Alma replied. "They don't get along so well with each other."

"Sheriff Fox is a challenge for anybody--even us--to get along with," Isabel said.

Isabel, Alma, and Farrah took their seats at the round table in her beauty shop. The refrigerator, sink, and microwave furnished the break room. The homespun aroma of buttered popcorn pervaded the space. Flaked out for his nap, Petey Samson occupied the fourth chair Isabel had dragged up to the table. She gave him an affectionate pat on the top of his head. His wagging tail was like a person's grateful smile.

Isabel gauged the wiry Farrah was in her mid-to-late forties. She preferred loose-fitting smocks, usually plum or pink, and white nurses' shoes since she spent the workday hustling about the shop. Her shiny, raven-black hair woven into a single plait spilled down her back. Her alert blue eyes never missed catching a detail, and she topped out an inch taller than Alma.

"I've been seriously thinking about closing up my beauty shop." Farrah looked glum and sounded downbeat. "Who'll come in after what happened to Laura?"

"My first reaction is don't shut it," Isabel replied. "But I can understand your reasons if you decide to go through with it."

Farrah's eyes fell on Alma. "Will you still come if I reopen it?"

Alma nodded. "Absolutely, I'll be back. I'll feel sad over the tragic loss of Laura, but her murder doesn't deter or scare me. We should get on with living our lives the way she'd expect us to do."

"You may count on our continued business," Isabel said.

"Thanks for giving me your helpful feedback," Farrah said.

"Maybe you could give me a trim now," Alma said. "We'll talk while you style my hair at a station mirror. Work is an excellent therapy for taking your mind off your troubles. What do you say?"

Isabel couldn't say anything because her jaw had dropped, hitting the table.

"Close your mouth unless you plan to catch flies, Isabel," Alma said as she wiggled her eyebrows.

Farrah didn't miss it and had to laugh. "I can see what you're doing. You think you can trick me into cutting your hair, so I'll feel more like hanging out my Come In, We're Open sign tomorrow."

Alma shrugged, her smile guileful. "Tell us about yesterday morning."

Farrah scowled. "It's by far the worst day of my life."

"Give us as much information as you feel up to sharing," Isabel said. "You'd parked your car around back, unlocked the alleyway door, and then you entered--."

"I parked on Main Street and came in the front door as my customers do," Farrah said. "The other merchants use their alleyway doors as entrances, but mine is strictly an emergency exit."

"What's in the rear alleyway?" Isabel asked.

"I keep the trash dumpster back there," Farrah replied.

"Can a person navigate down it at night?" Isabel asked.

"I had an exterior light installed for security reasons," Farrah replied.

"Tell us more about finding Laura," Isabel said. "Take your time. Alma and I have all day. Don't we, Alma?"

"I may have to make a sweet tooth run to Eddy's Deli," Alma replied.

"A box of chocolate-covered doughnuts is in the fridge," Farrah said. "Would you like me to get them out?"

"Perking a pot of coffee to wash them down would be marvelous, too," Alma replied. "Do you grind your own coffee beans? Do you use filtered or spring water? Do you have any creamer and sugar cubes on hand?"

"Alma, we came to hear Farrah's story," Isabel said. "Your coffee break will have to wait."

"Party pooper," Alma said. "Go ahead, Farrah. We're listening."

"I already covered this material with Deputy Sheriff Bexley," Farrah said.

"We'd like you to repeat your story to us," Isabel said. "Deputy Sheriff Bexley has the bad habit of forgetting the important details."

Farrah bit on her thumbnail as she drew on her memories. "I didn't notice Laura lying on the floor until after I left the break room. I ran over, knelt, and felt her wrist checking for a pulse, which wasn't there. She'd been dead for some time. So, I called the station house and spoke to Abigail."

Isabel nodded. "Abigail is the right person to contact."

"She's the only adult working for the sheriff," Alma said.

Again, Isabel nodded.

"My numb brain processed the startling fact somebody had killed Laura, and I was losing it. My palms broke out in a sweat. My heartbeats felt wobbly in my chest, and the blood rushed down from my face." Farrah glanced at Alma. "Do you ever feel that way?"

"Not since I got through menopause," Alma replied. "Isabel?"

"Are you kidding? Mine never went away," Isabel replied. "Had Laura's pocketbook been ransacked? Was her wallet taken out? Were her cash and credit cards missing?"

"Her pocketbook lay on her styling station table where I assume she'd set it down," Farrah replied. "Nobody had rifled through it. She wasn't killed during a botched robbery."

"Was Sheriff Fox the first authority you saw?" Isabel said.

"He found me sitting in here waiting," Farrah replied. "We talked for several minutes until the others arrived. He said he wanted to contact you since he knew murder mysteries are your specialty."

"Did he put up any yellow crime scene tape?" Alma asked.

"Did he ever," Farrah replied. "He unfurled *three* strands to cordon off the crime scene. I thought he was going overboard. When I told him so, he claimed using lots of yellow crime scene tape brings him good luck."

"What a ditzy man," Alma said, recalling the rabbit's foot she carried in her pocketbook.

"I made him take it down after he finished," Farrah said.

"If Laura's assailant hid in here, they'd remain out of sight until they were set to pounce on her," Isabel said.

"It's 20/20 hindsight, but I should've had surveillance cameras put up at the front and rear entrances," Farrah said.

"The surveillance video taken might've revealed something of interest," Isabel said.

"On the other hand, the video is often so grainy and blurred I doubt if we could use it," Alma said.

Isabel took a shrewd turn. "How did things stand between Laura and you, Farrah?"

"Despite everything, I'd say we got along civilly enough with each other," Farrah replied.

"Do I detect some tension and conflict between you and her?" Isabel asked.

"Oh, we fussed over nitpicky stuff," Farrah replied, waving a dismissive hand. "We never did it in front of the other hairstylists."

"Did your fights grow loud and heated?" Isabel said. "Did she push you to the brink of losing your temper?"

"We acted like two mature adults while calmly settling our differences," Farrah replied.

"Did you threaten to discipline or fire her if she didn't shape up?" Isabel asked.

"Things never got that out of hand," Farrah replied. "Once Laura understood what I expected from her, we had no further problems."

"What types of things caused friction between you?" Isabel asked.

"We had trivial issues, you know, like she didn't sweep up the hair clippings quickly enough, insisted on playing loud rock music, and refused to launder the towels during our slow periods," Farrah replied.

"Maybe things going on in her personal life distracted her," Isabel said.

"Laura was a paid professional," Farrah said. "I expected her to perform like one. Anyway, you both seemed happy with using her as your hairstylist."

Alma nodded.

"Did you see her socially outside the workplace?" Isabel asked. "Maybe you had an espresso or ate lunch while you were out together."

"Laura worked for me, and we had a cordial relationship. That's how I wanted to keep it," Farrah replied. "For one thing, I was considerably older, and we had nothing in common aside from the fact we both cut hair for a living."

"Did you offer her medical insurance since she worked for you full time?" Isabel asked.

"She got medical insurance for Deacon and her through me," Farrah replied. "I do my best to treat my employees right, especially since the new hair salons and spas have popped up in the strip malls and increased the competition. I'm aware enough to know competent hairstylists don't grow on trees."

"Did Laura threaten to leave you and go work at one of the new hair salons or spas?" Isabel asked.

"I heard the rumor from one of the other hairstylists," Farrah replied. "I'd be lying if I didn't tell you I felt hurt and betrayed by it. This Christmas I made enough profit to issue bonuses for the first time. Everybody seemed happy receiving them, including Laura."

"Did you confront her about what you'd heard?" Isabel asked. "Did you quarrel over it?"

"My making it into an issue wasn't appropriate," Farrah replied. "She was perfectly within her rights to leave here if she wished to go."

"Would you have offered her more money if she turned in her two-week notice?" Isabel asked.

"I couldn't afford to remain in business if I did," Farrah replied.

"Why did you give Laura a door key to open up the beauty shop?" Isabel asked.

"She wanted to come in early so she could leave early," Farrah replied. "I accommodated her, and I trusted her enough to take care of the opening. I didn't want to lose her, so I granted her request."

"Did she give up on her plan to leave you?" Isabel asked.

"The galling whispers continued in the beauty shop," Farrah replied.

"Did you stew over them?" Isabel asked. "Did you let them get under your skin? Did you lash out in a fit of fury to put a stop to them?"

"They exasperated and infuriated me," Farrah replied. "But I never discussed them with Laura. I had my pride, you see."

"Did you kill Laura Isherwood?" Isabel asked outright.

"Of course I didn't," Farrah replied, her tone firm and sure. "Why would I want to kill the goose that laid the golden egg? She was a pivotal part of my success."

Petey Samson yawned, stretched his legs, and gave Isabel his pinched stare.

"Nature beckons Petey Samson," Isabel said. "We should be leaving, too. Thanks for taking the time to see us and putting up with our nosy questions."

"Our meetings are never any bother," Farrah said. "I can only dust the retail shelves and change the light bulbs so many times."

"You might go home and try to decompress," Isabel said. "Sipping hot green tea and listening to jazz do wonders to relieve my stress."

"First I better shape up plans to reopen soon," Farrah said. "What other sensible choice do I have but to plug on with my business?"

"You go, girl," Alma said.

"Say again?" Farrah said.

"I used a popular expression," Alma replied.

"How odd," Farrah said.

"We'll be in touch by the day's end," Isabel said. "Take care of yourself. Come along, Alma. Time is awasting."

Petey Samson, barking his approval of Isabel's decision, was the first one bounding out the door. Alma holding the leash followed him. Just then, Farrah's grandfather clock tolled the hour in its deep-throated bongs, spurring Isabel to quicken her steps.

Chapter 7

Isabel hired an all-women lawn service crew of three to mow the grass and edge the sidewalk borders each week. Their lazy neighbor across the street, however, didn't cut his grass unless it was for a special occasion like when he invited over his poker night buddies, or when his parents drove up from Tampa for a visit. Alma proposed they stake a Please Mow Me! sign in his yard. Isabel said they'd wait until the grass reached their chins.

Isabel decided they should contact their youngest sister Louise who lived in a not-so-distant city. Isabel delegated making the phone call to Alma because the older sisters are often bossy. Alma didn't mind. She liked to get the latest scuttlebutt from Louise, which Alma might or might not share with Isabel because the younger sisters are just as often contrary.

"Who was Laura Isherwood?" Louise asked after Alma laid out their new mystery. "Was she a foreigner?"

"I'm uncertain if she was a townie native," Alma replied. "What difference does it make? Somebody murdered her, and that's what matters for us."

"She styled your hair, you say."

"Isabel and I preferred to book our hair appointments with Laura. She gave us an attractive cut, and we tipped her accordingly."

"Could one of her disgruntled customers have done her in?"

Alma took down her smartphone from her ear and peered at it. Had Louise been sipping Uncle Jimbo's brown jug? Its alcoholic contents were her nerve medicine, and he sent her a full brown jug when she ran empty. Alma was also known to partake of his brown jug to soothe her jangled nerves. Isabel proclaimed her lips never touched it. However, the contents of the brown jug Alma stored in her bedroom closet kept mysteriously going down. She suspected evaporation wasn't the cause as Isabel had said before she hiccupped.

"If a customer is displeased with a haircut, they go to a different beauty shop and try a different stylist," Alma replied. "They don't bump off the offending hairdresser."

"Doesn't it depend on how wretched the haircut looks, and how the customer reacts to it?" Louise asked. "At any rate, was Laura married, and did she have any children?"

"Deacon was her spouse, and they'd no children."

"Have you had a conversation with this Deacon?"

"We have and, of course, he denies he played any role in Laura's murder."

"You survived two bad marriages. What does your gut tell you about the Isherwoods? Was everything lovey-dovey, or did they have a rocky union?"

"If you're asking me whether I like Deacon, I'll tell you he makes my skin crawl."

"Then I'd trust my instincts and take a closer look at the creepy Deacon."

"You make it sound as if you think he has Laura's blood on his hands."

"Who else had a better opportunity to set up the murder? Who else more often murders a married victim than the spouse?"

"You make good points. Are you binge-reading mysteries?"

"Binge reading mysteries is my life. I bought a small shopping cart with a squeaky wheel to trundle around the public library. I fill it overflowing with borrowed mysteries. The librarians know me on a first-name basis, and they alert me about the newly published titles."

"You go to an awful lot of hassle. Have you ever thought of switching to an e-reader? I have one, and I love it."

"I haven't bought one because I like to take my time while cozying up to these newfangled gizmos."

"The e-readers have been out for a good while, but I like your cautious approach."

"How is your pooch faring?"

"Petey Samson is as much a rascal as he ever was, and we love him just the same. How's your rheumatoid arthritis treating you?"

"My rheumatologist informed me I won't be jumping through any fire-ringed hoops or bungee jumping from any hot air balloons."

"What a pity and shame except you never did that stuff anyway."

"I might ask our niece Megan to drive me down to Quiet Anchorage to call on you gals. How does my idea grab you?"

"You're always welcome here. Seeing your hometown and old friends again will perk up your spirits. Just give me a call when you plan to come. If Sheriff Fox is blindsided with the news all three Trumbo sisters are in town, I don't know what might happen to him.

A heart attack or mental breakdown isn't outside the realm of possibilities."

"I'll give you enough lead time to prepare Roscoe for my return. Should I wait until you're not working on a case?"

"Come when you're ready since I don't see any letup down the road. If we're on a case when you arrive, you can pitch in. The sleuth DNA must be embedded in your genes as it is in ours."

"Then let's plan on it, and I'll phone you later with the specifics," Louise said.

"I can't wait to share the good news with Isabel," Alma said. "Bye for now."

After hearing the latest news from Louise, Isabel drove her and Alma to the Dunfee Sash and Door Company in Culpeper. Laura's husband Deacon worked there as a forklift operator, but he'd taken his bereavement leave and wouldn't see them. They'd use the pretense they were gathering price quotes on the installation of new windows in their brick rambler. They came armed with a slate of questions, including a few nosy ones having nothing to do with windows.

The cavernous Dunfee Sash and Door warehouse constructed of prefabricated metal had a sloped roof. Slippery elms shaded each side of the detached brick building with the Office sign over the door. Isabel eased into the parking space by a champagne-colored Range Rover, which she suspected belonged to Mr. Dunfee.

"Wish us luck," Isabel said.

"My stomach is growling," Alma said. "I must've eaten the emergency moon pie I keep in the glove compartment. Did you happen to bring one?"

Isabel shook her head. "First we interview Mr. Dunfee, and then we'll see about getting lunch."

"Your priorities are out of whack if you ask me."

"Do you expect me to make a moon pie run to the nearest convenience store just because your stomach is growling?"

"Would it be the end of the world if you did? My sweet tooth is raging out of control."

Isabel frowned. "Quit dreaming of moon pies and knuckle down on getting to the bottom of Laura's murder mystery."

"Don't fret about me. I'll just suffer in silence while I wait for my moon pie."

"Jessica Fletcher never worried about her next lobster dinner while she sleuthed in Cabot Cove," Isabel said.

"How can you compare eating a lowly crustacean to a yummy moon pie?" Alma said.

"Alma, you're starting to ruffle my feathers," Isabel said.

"Maybe we should break up the Trumbo sisters team," Alma said. "We'll each become a separate sleuth and investigate our own cases."

Isabel laughed. "You wouldn't last a day working by yourself on a case."

"I can do it every bit as well as you can," Alma said. "Who would ever suspect a short, dumpy lady is a master sleuth?"

"Quit acting like a nincompoop," Isabel said. "We're meant to work together as partners like Laverne and Shirley or Lucy and Ethel."

"Have it your way then," Alma said. "What I think doesn't count."

Isabel used every ounce of her self-control to keep from rolling her eyes, but she failed.

Mr. Dunfee kept his office comfortable for a polar bear. Isabel didn't know what it was about the men who insisted on lowering the thermostat. Clenching her teeth prevented them from chattering. A tall man skinny as a zipper striding out from the back room focused on them.

Seeing no office administrator, Isabel concluded Mr. Dunfee did everything. Maybe he brought in an office temp if things turned busy. Her suspicion he was a tightwad left her with a negative opinion of him. Closer up, he switched on a smile phony as a plastic banana.

"Welcome to the Dunfee Sash and Door Company. Sidney Dunfee is at your service. Just call me Stretch. How might I help you, ladies?"

"I'm Alma, and she's my sister Isabel," Alma replied. "We drove down to check out your line of windows, Stretch."

"Then you came to the right place, Isabel and Alma," Stretch said. "Why are you in the market for new windows?"

"The windows in our house are wobbly wrecks," Alma replied. "Many of them won't go up without applying a few whacks from a rolling pin or a frying pan. We've sealed the cracked panes with duct tape, but the winter drafts still leak indoors. We've been postponing it for too long, but now we're set to fix them before the first frost hits."

"Are you also looking to install window screens?" Stretch asked.

"Window screens are nice," Alma replied. "Isabel and I aren't fond of sharing our living quarters with spiders, horseflies, and stink bugs."

"Nor am I," Stretch said. "The window screens will run you a little extra, but they're worth the investment."

"Aren't the window screens included with the basic window price?" Isabel asked. "I saw them advertised that way on your competitors' websites."

"Yes, the window screens are included now that you mention it." Stretch chuckled. "It must've slipped my mind. Sorry. I need to drink more of my bad coffee and wake up."

Isabel glanced at the also skeptical Alma.

"Where are you ladies from?" Stretch asked.

"We hail from Quiet Anchorage," Isabel replied. "Do you know where it is?"

"I've driven through it numerous times over the years," Stretch replied. "However, I never stop there. Isn't it a dangerous spot?"

"We've had one or maybe two murders take place if that concerns you," Alma replied.

"One or maybe two murders is a gross understatement," Stretch said.

Alma bristled with indignation. "Quiet Anchorage is our hometown. Is it a bad neighborhood where you don't want to send your delivery truck?"

"I wasn't disparaging your hometown," Stretch replied. "One of my employees is from there."

"Who might that be?" Alma asked.

"Deacon Isherwood," Stretch replied. "Ever heard of him?"

"He's not a stranger to us," Alma said.

"Then you must've heard what happened to his wife Laura yesterday morning," Stretch said.

Alma nodded with no vocal response. She wanted to keep Stretch talking about Laura's murder.

"I don't know what the world has come to if you can't go to your job and not feel safe there," Stretch said. "Did you happen to know Laura?"

"She was our hairstylist for several years," Alma replied.

"Folks say she was a fine one and very much in demand," Stretch said.

"How's Deacon handling her murder?" Alma asked.

"I sent him home yesterday morning," Stretch replied. "I haven't heard a word from him since. I imagine he's busy making the funeral arrangements."

Alma didn't point out Deacon was busy watching TV and playing Solitaire. She also didn't reveal he was one of their murder suspects.

"Are you ladies ready to take a tour of the window models display room?" Stretch's hand showed them the way.

"Is it next to the penguin cage?" Alma asked.

"I beg your pardon?" Stretch said.

"It's nothing," Isabel said. "What were you saying?"

"I'll give you my personal guided tour," Stretch replied.

"Have you any summer sales or special deals going for your preferred customers?" Alma asked.

"I don't offer my preferred customers any summer sales or special deals since my everyday prices are rock bottom," Stretch replied. "If I knocked off even a few cents, I'd be losing money, and my employees deserve to make a living wage."

"No question about it, you have to make money on your end, too," Isabel said.

"We're not rolling in dough," Alma said. "As you may have noticed when Isabel pulled up, we don't own a Cadillac or Porch."

"It's called a Porsche, not a Porch, Alma." Isabel laughed. "You'll make Mr. Dunfee think we're a pair of country bumpkins who just fell off the tater truck."

Stretch chuckled.

"Oops, my boo-boo," Alma said. "Mr. Dunfee must think I'm not hitting on all my cylinders." She smiled at the pun.

"I understand what you're telling me," Stretch said. "Seniors live on fixed incomes and have to pinch their pennies to make ends meet."

"We pinch our pennies so tightly our thumbprints are left on them," Alma said.

Stretch chuckled. "You ladies have a wonderfully dry sense of humor."

"You bet, Stretch," Alma said. "We're just a laugh a minute."

Again, Stretch chuckled.

"Have you had your company picnic this summer?" Isabel asked.

"I held it on June fourth in the grassy lot behind the warehouse," Stretch replied. "A bluegrass band picked a few tunes while the caterer served the tastiest barbecued pulled pork on this side of the Blue Ridge Mountains. Everybody said they had a magnificent time, so I plan to do it again next summer."

"We love barbecued pulled pork and bluegrass music," Isabel said. "Did your employees bring their spouses?"

"I encourage them to bring their spouses and kids," Stretch replied. "We put on a family event with good, clean fun for all, young and old alike."

"Did Deacon show up on June fourth?" Isabel asked.

"Sure, he was there," Stretch replied. "He's never missed a company picnic as far as I can remember."

"Was Laura with him?" Isabel asked.

"She didn't accompany him this summer," Stretch replied.

"Did he give you a reason for her absence?" Isabel asked.

"When I asked him, I think he said she had a sinus headache or something of that nature," Stretch replied.

"You'd think he'd stay home and take care of his sick wife instead of traipsing off to a company picnic," Isabel said.

Stretch nodded. "My wife Robin Lou told me the same thing. Laura had come to our previous picnics, and we loved seeing her. She was so full of energy and humor."

"You don't have to tell us," Alma said.

"Was she popular with the other wives?" Isabel asked.

"She easily mingled with everybody." Stretch gave them a curious look. "Why are you asking me so many questions about Deacon, Laura, and our company picnic?"

"Alma and I are shameless gossips keeping an ear out for any idle chitchat," Isabel replied, playing fast and loose with the truth as the sleuths often do while plying their trade. "We're like sponges soaking up the tidbits about what goes on in Quiet Anchorage. Nothing is too trivial or mundane for our consumption."

Stretch grinned. "How could I have forgotten how you older ladies are?"

"We can't help our nosiness," Isabel said. "It's like an addiction."

"I saw Deacon offer the master barbecuer a few tips on how to grill the pork, and he got a stony glare for his trouble," Stretch said. "If you're smart, you don't commit such a picnic faux pas."

"Master barbecuers are touchy about getting any constructive criticism," Alma said. "I'd be careful offering it if they're wielding a two-prong meat fork or a meat cleaver."

"That's solid advice to heed," Stretch said.

"Since it's so close to lunchtime, why don't we go on and run our errands?" Isabel said. "We'll swing by Stretch's salesroom later and take our time selecting which of his window models is the right one for us."

"Is that agreeable with you, Stretch?" Alma asked.

"I'll spend all the time I need with you good ladies," Stretch replied. "I treat my customers like they're family. I've won service awards, which I hang on my office wall. Be advised we accept personal checks drawn on local banks and major credit cards."

"Do you accept cold hard cash on the barrelhead?" Alma asked.

"That goes without saying," Stretch replied.

"Somehow I thought it might," Alma said. "Thanks for talking to us."

"Here, take one of my business cards," Stretch said, offering it.

"Thanks, but I can remember your phone number when I need to use it," Alma said.

Chapter 8

"We aren't too shabby for a couple of amateurs if I may brag a little." Alma was munching on her moon pie. "As just two little old aunties from a small town, we haven't lost our shamus touch."

"What are you babbling about now?" Isabel asked.

"We interviewed Stretch without his catching on how we were mining him for information."

"You make us out to be sneaky and predatory. We asked him a few pertinent questions, and he was free to send us on our way if he didn't wish to answer them."

"It was like taking candy from a baby,"

"Aren't you feeling cocky and full of yourself?"

"The power of positive thinking is an amazing force, Isabel."

On the way home, they stopped and browsed at a quilts shop in Brandy Station. An enterprising lady sewed the quilts in her home and displayed them for sale in the bright, airy front room, what Isabel and Alma's mother Gwendolyn had called the sitting parlor.

Shopping for winter quilts in the summertime struck Alma as a bit kooky, but she went along with Isabel's whim. She thought if the quilts lady had discounted her wares, they might score a bargain. Alma pointed out they needed to shop for *two* quilts, one to cover each of their beds, and Isabel was twice as happy. The quilts display room had a cinnamony smell like from hot sticky buns.

Alma paused in front of a graveyard quilt--hung up for display purposes only and not for sale--and admired its intricate design. Isabel checked around them for any other browsers. They were alone and safe.

"So, Deacon didn't bring Laura with him to the company picnic this summer," Isabel said.

"Everything wasn't going so smoothly under the Isherwoods' roof," Alma said. "Deacon and Laura had a quarrel or dispute, and they couldn't patch it up in time for attending the company picnic."

"Deacon gave Stretch the excuse Laura stayed home sick with a sinus headache," Isabel replied. "Deacon may have been telling the truth. She was feeling under the weather and didn't feel up to it."

"Then why didn't he stay home and take care of her?" Alma asked. "Wouldn't he be too worried about her to enjoy being at the company picnic?"

"If he was worth a plug nickel, you'd think so," Isabel replied.

Alma turned her attention back to the graveyard quilt hanging from the quilt clamps adhered to the wall. The gallery track lighting mounted on the ceiling beamed down, illuminating the quilt's rich details: marble tombstones, a wrought iron fence, and a grove of crepe myrtle trees. Their crimson blooms added a dash of color. A clematis vine paired with a climbing rose festooned the wrought iron fence with indigo blue and peppermint white flowers.

Alma couldn't remember the last time they'd visited the town cemetery and tended to Gwendolyn and Woodrow's marble grave markers. Was it on Decoration Day this past May? They'd packed a picnic lunch and brought whatever yard flowers were in season to set out on their parents' gravesites.

It was a reflective occasion. Humming the lyrics to the gospel song "I'll Fly Away," Alma raked up the leaves and twigs from the gravesites. Meanwhile, Isabel spent a few quiet minutes alone where her late husband Max and son Cecil lay side by side in repose under a flowering dogwood. She'd never tell a soul how much she missed them, and she didn't have the adequate words even if she wanted to describe it. Cecil, a two-packs-a-day smoker, had died before his time. Cancer sticks, she'd called them.

"Why does this graveyard quilt intrigue us so much?" Isabel asked.

"The quilt maker's patience and care astound me," Alma replied. "She must've sat for hours in her sunlit rocker while she sewed together the fabric pieces before she added the batting and backing. How many times did she pause with the sewing needle and deliberate over what quilting step should come next?"

"I'd never find the perseverance to sew a quilt of this size. Was she in mourning for a loved one's death, and sewing it was her therapy?"

Alma smiled. "Maybe between sewing her quilt and reading her bible verses, she remained the iron-willed matriarch who held her family together through the distressing times."

Isabel nodded. "You know, Farrah had the best opportunity to set up the murder. She could've arrived earlier than Laura at the beauty shop and remained out of sight until the right moment came to strike."

"But as Laura's family members, hubbie Deacon or sister Jodie would have the stronger passion to murder her," Alma said. "Laura was on agreeable terms with Jodie but not so much with Deacon."

"Is Deacon, then, her killer?" Isabel asked. "Should we give him our closest attention for now?"

"He's running on the inside track," Alma replied.

Isabel turned wistful. "I'm not in a quilt-buying mood when I step outdoors, and it's ninety degrees blasting me in the face. None of the price tags offer a hot-weather discount."

"We could haggle a better price on the quilts we like. She probably expects us to dicker with her anyway."

"I can't bring myself to after we know how much of her heart and soul she poured into each quilt."

"I wouldn't feel right if we did, either. However, she's priced the quilts a little above our range," Alma said.

"She'll probably offer a larger selection for sale this autumn, and we'll feel less guilty about shelling out so much money," Isabel said.

"Good afternoon, ladies," a different lady's voice rasped from behind them. "I was in the back canning the string beans I'd picked and didn't hear you come in. Welcome to my humble abode. Folks call me Quillie, short for Quillian as well as my zest to quilt as you can observe."

Short and squat, Quillie padded out a faded rose-print dress. She schlepped into the display room, her tennis shoes pink with untied yellow shoelaces. Bobby pins held her coppery red hair pulled back into a lopsided bunch. She mauled a wad of gum and wore a pair of vintage cat-eye glasses on the bridge of her nose.

Smiling, Isabel introduced her and Alma to Quillie. "Did you sew all of these quilts?"

"Every one of them is mine except for the graveyard quilt," Quillie replied.

"We stand in awe of your prodigious talent and ambition," Alma said.

"It's just a little thing I do to stay out of trouble," Quillie said, deflecting the compliment.

"Where did you get this gorgeous graveyard quilt?" Isabel asked.

"It got passed down through the different generations of Custalows until it landed there on my wall," Quillie replied. "Isn't it something else?"

"It's an absolute gem," Alma replied.

"Are the brown quilt pieces made of calico?" Isabel asked.

"Yes, indeed, they are," Quillie replied. "My forbearer, her name was Daisy Mae, made the brown dye from the walnut hulls she collected. She included other ingredients, of course, but she took her dyeing processes to the grave."

"Do you name your quilts like after a favorite dish or place?" Isabel asked.

"I'm not like many of my fellow quilters," Quillie replied. "To me, they're just stunning quilts and not living, breathing organisms worthy of giving names."

"We've taken up enough of your time," Isabel said. "Thank you for showing us your unforgettable exhibition."

"You're more than welcome." Quillie narrowed her eyes as her entrepreneurial streak showed. "Can I interest you in buying one of them?"

"Alma and I discussed it before you walked in," Isabel replied. "We plan to return soon after Labor Day and purchase not one but *two* of your quilts. I assume you'll still be open in September."

Quillie had a rusty laugh. "I have no plans to be anywhere else. Come any time after eight o'clock. First, I have to feed Harlan breakfast and bundle him off to work. He drives a dump truck at the phosphate quarry. Then I'm free as a bird for the rest of the day to quilt away to my heart's delight."

"Fair enough, Quillie," Alma replied. "Be looking for us soon after Labor Day."

"Or we'll return sooner if the right mood strikes us," Isabel said.

⊷ ⊷ ⊷

Fredo's Frozen Custard on Main Street across from the Azul Lago Florist Shop and next door to an antique shop had been in operation for about a year. The line of customers often snaked halfway down the block, especially on summer evenings. He also sold a half-dozen flavors of Italian ice as well as sweet treats like baklava, key lime pie, and red velvet cake. He was a popular man in town.

"I do declare, Isabel." Alma used her derisive schoolmarm voice. "I've had a hankering for a frozen custard cone since Mr. Mockingbird woke me up at the crack of dawn. How about you?"

"It will spoil your dinner," Isabel replied as she made the turn on Main Street.

"Yes, Mother, I know that, but I want it just the same. Why are we having this argument? I can see you're on your way to Fredo's Frozen Custard."

"I'm headed there before you fling one of your fuzzy-tailed conniptions. You can order whatever you wish. I'll remain in the car and solve the rest of my crossword puzzle while I wait for you."

"You will, huh? I say fat chance."

"Correct me if I'm wrong, but did you in so many words just dare me?"

"I dare you to resist the temptation to go in with me and buy your usual treat."

Isabel parked at the front door. She opened the door latch and glanced back at Alma.

"What are you waiting for?" Isabel asked. "Let's order our goodies so we can get back to work."

Alma grinned. "Are you paying for them?"

"And you can the next time. Do you have the yen for chocolate or strawberry?"

"I'll decide when I place my order."

"Is that Phyllis Garner waving at us through the window?"

"It sure is. This day just keeps getting better and better."

Isabel and Alma paced into Fredo's Frozen Custards where, as Isabel suspected, the air conditioner roared away.

"I may have to order a hot fudge sundae and a steamy cup of coffee," Alma said, warding off a shudder.

"Should I go back to the car and grab our sweaters before we grow icicles on the tips of our noses?" Isabel asked.

"We'll tough it out." Alma motioned with her chin toward the window table. "I'm bursting with curiosity to hear the latest word from Phyllis."

"She always knows something juicy," Isabel said.

Isabel paid the young attendant for the chocolate frozen custard scoops piled on sugar cones. They left the counter. Phyllis Garner dressed as an eccentric bag lady although by now most of the townies knew she was faking it. She was an outspoken woman who enjoyed laughing. Sammi Jo had a full-time job keeping a close eye on her unpredictable, unflappable Aunt Phyllis. This afternoon she was attired in a sleeveless yellow sundress, low platform sandals, and a wide-brim floppy straw hat.

"Your bright yellow outfit makes me think of a giant canary," Alma said.

"That's the quirky look I was going for," Phyllis said. "Why don't you take a load off, and we'll chew the fat awhile?"

"We don't mind if we do," Isabel replied as they settled into the chairs facing Phyllis.

"Tell me everything," Phyllis said. "Sammi Jo called and said you've put on your gumshoes again, but she was skimpy on the details."

"At Sheriff Fox's request, we've been checking into the Laura Isherwood homicide," Isabel said.

"You'd do it even if he hadn't asked you," Phyllis said.

"We discovered the hard way it's better to get him involved from the get-go," Isabel said. "After all, we're the amateurs."

"You as the amateurs can run circles around the so-called professionals like him," Phyllis said.

"Thanks for your vote of confidence," Isabel said.

"Quite so. You made our day," Alma said.

"Be quick and eat your frozen custard before it melts even if it is cold as a well digger's shovel in here," Phyllis said.

"What town chatter have you heard, Phyllis?" Isabel asked. "Have any names arisen in the speculations made about who killed Laura Isherwood?"

"One-third of the townies says her hubby Deacon did it, the second third insists it was her boss Farrah, and the last third claims her sister Jodie is the culprit," Phyllis replied. "Take your pick of which one you believe is guilty."

"If you had to cast a vote, how would you call it?" Alma asked.

"I'd give Deacon my special attention because he didn't get along with Laura," Phyllis replied.

"Is that what the town grapevine says?" Isabel asked.

"It's what Phyllis Garner says," Phyllis replied. "I saw them quarreling in the bank parking lot earlier this summer."

"Did their heated altercation turn physical?" Isabel asked.

"Loud words and angry cursing were all I witnessed," Phyllis replied. "Who does Sheriff Fox think is the killer?"

"Who gives a hoot in a boot?" Alma replied. "He always hangs back until Isabel and I figure out who the guilty party is, and then he swoops in like the hero of the hour to make the arrest."

"Where else but in Quiet Anchorage could it end like that?" Phyllis asked.

"We retired ladies don't have to worry about such responsibilities as work and family," Alma replied. "We're free to pursue our sleuthing activities around the clock if we wish."

"It's never been my wish," Isabel said. "If it happens after nine p.m., you'd better forget about it until the next morning, and then it's only after seven a.m. I need to get my beauty rest and my first cup of coffee."

"Don't let her fool you for one second," Alma said. "Isabel is always eager to pursue our detective work."

"I'll keep my ears and eyes open and pass along anything I learn," Phyllis said. "Your phone numbers are on my speed dial."

"You're the best, Phyllis," Isabel said. "Come along, Alma. We've grown too lax this afternoon, and it's time for us to grab another gear, as Reynolds Kyle would say."

"He's sending Sammi Jo to the nuthouse with his skittish nerves, fast talk, and cold feet," Phyllis said.

"She's vowed to corner him when he gets home and pin him down to set their wedding date," Alma said.

"He's too slippery and evasive to pin down," Phyllis said.

"Sammi Jo has to learn it on her own," Alma said.

"He'd better not break her young heart is all I can say," Phyllis said. "Or else he'll have to contend with my wrath."

"I wouldn't envy him in those dire straits," Isabel replied.

Chapter 9

Later on, they huddled together in a window booth at Eddy's Deli. Everybody ordered a tall glass of iced tea, and Alma polished off "a slice of heaven to tide me over until dinnertime." Isabel sent Sammi Jo an amused glance as Alma devoured her cherry pie wedge, and nobody said anything. Sammi Jo's stalled wedding plans were the current topic under consideration.

"I haven't received one text or phone call from Reynolds since he hit the Darlington Raceway with his gearhead cronies," Sammi Jo said.

"He probably knows better," Alma said. "If he did call you, he'd hear you read him the riot act."

Isabel nodded.

"Something has to give," Sammi Jo said. "I can't go on doing this back and forth dance with him. Either we're getting married, or we're not. We have to render a final decision."

"Perhaps Reynolds hasn't given it enough thought and needs more time," Isabel said.

"More time? He's had forever and a day to mull it over," Sammi Jo said. "Does he expect me to wait around forever? I'm almost twenty-three and not a spring chicken. I don't want to end up as a crazy old spinster clad in a moth-eaten cardigan and trapped in a ramshackle bungalow with black crepe drapes, Venus flytraps, and Mynah birds."

Isabel and Alma sighed.

"Consider laying an ultimatum on him," Alma said. "Make sure he understands this one is final and binding. He won't get another chance to decide."

"Sammi Jo tried that ploy once, and it went bust," Isabel said.

"I'd forgotten it fizzled out," Alma said. "Scuttle my idea then."

"Have you been carrying the family heirloom we gave you?" Isabel asked.

"It goes everywhere with me," Sammi Jo replied. "So far, I've felt nothing. Could its magic love powers have expired?"

"Mother didn't say it has a shelf life," Isabel replied.

"Keep it close to you," Alma said. "You never can tell when it might activate, and you'd better be ready for when it does."

Sammi Jo grinned. "I'll take anything it can give me, so I'll wait longer."

"Is Jodie holding back information she knows about Laura?" Isabel asked.

"Jodie seemed to act evasive," Alma replied.

"Maybe you didn't ask her the right questions," Sammi Jo said.

"We can't very well march into the office at Blevins Millworks and badger her," Alma said.

"I want more information on her divorce from Bernie Wright while they lived in Richmond," Isabel said.

"Sammi Jo can fire up her laptop computer, hop on gaggle, and run her searches," Alma said.

"I can hop on what?" Sammi Jo asked, her expression befuddled.

Isabel chuckled. "Alma means to say Google. For some reason, she can't remember the name of the search engine."

"I got it close enough so that you understood me," Alma said.

"Before Archie hired Jodie, did he ask her for job references?" Isabel asked.

"If she talked a good game during her interview, he was impressed enough to offer her the job without a background check," Sammi Jo replied. "Archie had mucked up things with the company ledgers, and only a bookkeeping wizard could straighten them out. All Jodie had to do was wave her magic wand and convince him she was the right wizard to bring in."

"How well do you know Archie?" Isabel asked.

"I do about as well as you do," Sammi Jo replied. "What's on your mind?"

"I'm looking for a pretense to buttonhole Archie in a private place and ask him about Jodie," Isabel replied.

"How inquisitive can you be?" Sammi Jo asked. "If he gets the notion you suspect his fabulous bookkeeper of murder, there's no telling how he might react."

Alma nodded. "He's thrilled with the work she's done, and he's not going to sit still and listen to us level a murder accusation against her."

"Then we'll hold off on seeing him for now," Isabel said.

"What possible motive did Jodie have?" Alma asked.

"Their sibling jealousy or rivalry may have culminated in murder." Isabel closed her eyes while exploring a new thought. "Did Jodie lie to us? Is she really in love with Deacon? Did she kill Laura to have him all to herself? Is it too outlandish and melodramatic to consider the scenario?"

"When it comes to murder, I see no limits on the types of motives there are," Alma replied.

"Honestly, I don't know what she, or any lady, sees in Deacon," Sammi Jo replied.

"I feel the same way," Alma said. "Care to make it a hat trick, Isabel?"

"Deacon doesn't give me a warm and fuzzy feeling," Isabel replied. "Branding him as the murderer just because we don't like him isn't fair. If the evidence incriminating him exists, we're under the obligation to produce it."

"Should we ask Blaine for his take on our conversation with Deacon?" Alma asked.

"Since they're longtime friends, I don't trust Blaine to give us a truthful response," Isabel replied.

"Surely, he won't cover for Deacon if he's a murderer," Alma said.

"We shouldn't have to ask Blaine or others what they think," Isabel said. "We'll make up our own minds."

"Shall we go from here and get the latest roundup from the Three Musketeers?" Alma asked.

"You know I value their inputs," Isabel replied.

"I thought you just said we don't need to get anybody's inputs to make up our minds," Sammi Jo said.

"Oh, come on, Sammi Jo. I'm always contradicting myself," Isabel said. "Haven't you learned that about me by now?"

"I know I sure have over the years," Alma said.

❧ ❧ ❧

The Three Musketeers, the gaffers occupying the wooden bench on Main Street, talked when not watching the world go by or sneaking in a catnap. They resembled craggy terrapins sunning themselves on a mossy log along the riverside. Corina had outlawed any spitting and cursing in front of her florist shop. Willie protested, but she wouldn't lift her ban. However, she hadn't said anything about discontinuing the pranks or jokes.

"Willie, in case you wondered, I had my attorney change my Last Will," Blue said. "You're to inherit two of my worldly possessions when I turn into worm food. I know it's disappointing, but you'll only receive my tube of stinky orange salve and my bedpan collection. Use them wisely and make them last, my friend."

"I'm not one whit interested, Blue, but thanks for keeping me apprised," Willie said. "Now, in case *you* were curious, I directed my attorney to scratch you altogether from my Last Will."

"Ossie, do you know anything about Willie cutting me out of his Last Will?" Blue asked.

"You're hearing it for the first time like I am," Ossie replied. "In case you both had any question, I never included either of you in my Last Will."

"I'd give you some guff about it," Blue said. "Except we can see Isabel, Alma, and Sammi Jo are on their way over here, and I'd much rather talk to them than to either of you cheapskates."

"We're hardly offended, Blue," Willie said. "The feeling is mutual, I can assure you."

The Three Musketeers turned to gaze in the same direction up the sidewalk.

"From their somber faces, I deduce they haven't wrapped up the Laura Isherwood murder case," Blue said.

"They'll ask us if we've heard anything new," Willie said. "We'll reply that we haven't since our discussion of our Last Wills has diverted our attention."

"I have one final thing to say on the subject," Ossie said. "Who's going to get your pot of money, Willie?"

"That information is top secret," Willie replied. "You'll find out after I bite the dust if you're still around."

Ossie glanced at Blue. "He's leaving his pot of money to the officials holding the UFO soirée each August in Roswell, New Mexico."

"I'm not shocked," Blue said. "Flying saucers and little green men are more important to Willie than his two best pals are."

"Flying saucers and little green men don't give me any back-sass like I get from you pair," Willie said. "By the way, who might you be leaving your pot of money to, Ossie?"

"Why, I'm taking mine with me," Ossie replied. "Who can predict? I might need to spend a few bucks after I sail through the pearly gates."

"Nobody can take their money with them when they shuffle off this mortal coil," Willie said. "What's the matter with you? Have you been eating those magic mushrooms?"

"I'll pack my greenbacks in a duffle bag and hitch a ride into the cosmos aboard one of your UFOs," Ossie said.

"That shows how little you know," Willie said. "UFOs never stop and pick up hitchhikers."

"How do you know?" Ossie asked. "Have you ever stuck your thumb out to flag one down?"

"I did once, and the UFO zipped right past me," Willie replied.

"If I'd been driving it, I would've run over you," Blue said.

"Tone it down, guys," Ossie said. "Our company has arrived."

Isabel greeted them. "Good afternoon, gentlemen. How are things going in your part of town?"

"We're staying alert for any new rumors," Ossie replied.

"We're akin to three radar dishes on the wooden bench," Willie said.

"Leave me out of the radar comparison," Ossie said. "I'm having nothing to do with it since I was nailed for a speeding ticket."

"Did you get one for doing 95 in a 55?" Willie asked.

"Deputy Sheriff Bexley dinged me for going 26 in a 25," Ossie replied.

"He's back to brown-nosing for his boss again," Willie said.

"Did Laura stop at the florist shop during her final week alive?" Alma asked.

"We rarely saw her walking on Main Street this summer," Ossie replied. "She spent most of her time working in the beauty shop."

"Didn't she usually visit the shopkeepers and run errands after work?" Isabel asked.

Ossie nodded. "We used to frequently see her smiling face, and I'm not sure why she stopped coming around."

"She got tired of putting up with the crotchety likes of you," Blue said.

Ossie gave his friend the fish eye. "I'm no more crotchety than you are, old-timer."

"Who are you calling an old-timer?" Ossie asked.

"We're veering off-topic," Willie replied. "The matter at hand is Laura's murder, not your personality flaws."

"I wonder if Laura was distraught over some trouble and had stopped going out in public," Isabel said.

"When did you last see her to get a haircut?" Alma asked.

"My salon appointment came three weeks ago," Isabel replied. "If she was angry or agitated, I missed seeing it. When was your most recent appointment with her?"

Alma fluffed her short gray hair. "I'd rather not admit when it was, but she didn't act any different to me."

"Speaking of haircuts, did I ever tell you I was a barber while I was in the army?" Blue asked. "I once gave a four-star general a hot shave with a straight razor, and I didn't nick him once."

"We don't care to hear your old army story," Ossie replied.

"That's okay," Blue said. "I'll save it for telling you later."

"I'm sure it's a real nail-biter," Ossie said.

"Ossie, on some days your cynicism is boorish and insufferable," Blue said. "Today is such a day."

"Did you get out early enough yesterday morning to see Laura open up the beauty shop?" Isabel asked.

"If it happened before breakfast, no Musketeer had graced the wooden bench with his presence," Willie replied.

"Have you noticed anybody unusual hanging around or going into the beauty shop lately?" Isabel asked.

"Farrah draws a lot of business from the new folks who've moved to the area," Willie replied. "We don't know them all and have given up trying to learn their names."

"They're just plain folks like we are," Isabel said. "We should make them feel welcome and extend our famous Virginia hospitality."

"Tell Willie about it and not us," Blue said. "He's been acting cranky as a bag of tomcats."

"You three old fellows had better be careful of how cranky you get, or folks might label you as"--here Isabel paused for dramatic emphasis--"as *curmudgeons*."

The Three Musketeers gasped together, their eyes widening in shock and horror.

"Curmudgeons? Who? Us?" Ossie gulped.

"The very thought of it curdles my blood," Blue said.

"Nobody wants to be branded as a curmudgeon," Willie said.

"I should think not," Isabel said. "Nobody shares the town gossip with one."

"Thanks for warning us," Ossie said. "I'll make sure we don't fall prey to curmudgeonhood."

"If anything is whispered on Main Street, we'll be sure to hear it," Willie said.

"If we're finished, I have to tell Ossie my old army story," Blue said.

"Stick around, ladies," Ossie said. "What's your hurry?"

"We've gotten what we need from you," Isabel replied. "We'll leave and let you enjoy listening to Blue."

"I can't wait to hear it," Ossie said. "Where are my earbuds?"

Chapter 10

After finishing their afternoon errands, they went home, and Isabel decided she'd read one of her mysteries until it was time to fix dinner. She'd save reading the cozy mysteries they kept in the home library until the wintertime to relish while she sipped her hot cups of green tea laced with lemon and clover honey. A slice of pound cake spread with strawberry jelly or date bread spread with butter made it even better.

She flipped open Margaret Millar's jewel of a private eye yarn *How Like an Angel* featuring Joe Quinn published in 1962. Isabel held the unshakeable opinion Ms. Millar gave the heralded male private eye writers Dashiell Hammett, Raymond Chandler, and even her husband Kenneth Millar (a.k.a. Ross Macdonald) a brisk run for their money.

After nestling in her broken-in armchair, Isabel adjusted her half-moon reading glasses and resumed following the tale. She took an occasional sip from the tall glass of iced tea on the end table. When her reading engrossed her, she attained a state of pure bliss and forbade any interruptions.

However, Petey Samson--the furry reprobate!--had different ideas. He waddled over to the coffee table, snatched up the dog leash in his mouth, and trotted over to Isabel where he dropped it on the carpet by her shoes. Isabel went on reading and ignored him.

However, Petey Samson was just getting started. He returned to the coffee table and grabbed Isabel's pair of sunglasses. This time he deposited them next to the dog leash. His look determined Isabel hadn't given him a cursory glance. More determined than ever, he continued his mission.

By now, Alma also sitting in her armchair had noticed Petey Samson. She watched his antics with an impish smile. He poked his muzzle into Isabel's pocketbook she'd left on the coffee table and scrounged around in quest of something. His tail wagged as he wrenched it out and gripped it in his mouth. He returned to Isabel and dropped her key ring next to the dog leash and sunglasses. He sat down, began panting, and beamed up his soulful brown eyes at her. Alma could barely stifle her snickers.

Woof-woof.

Isabel twitched her eyebrows, however, she finished reading the page and turned to the next one.

Woof-woof.

"Uh, Isabel, your hound dog, I think, wants your attention," Alma said. "Are you ignoring him on purpose? I don't believe he'll shush up and go away so easily."

Isabel heaved out a sigh as she regarded them. "Can't you see I'm reading my detective novel despite all the fuss? What is so urgent that it can't wait?"

"Look down by your shoes and see what Petey Samson has brought you," Alma replied.

Isabel observed his dog leash, her sunglasses, and her key ring on the carpet.

"Despite the fact I think I know the answer, I'll ask the question anyway," she said. "Why do I find these three items lying here?"

Woof-woof.

"No."

Woof-woof.

"I said, 'no.' Which word don't you understand?"

Woof-woof.

"You sure are feeling your oats today."

Woof-woof.

"I refuse to take you for a joyride in the car," Isabel said. "That's my final word, so don't you dare *woof-woof* and ask me again. No means no. Period. Full stop. End of discussion."

Woof-woof.

"I won't take you even if you say pretty please with sugar and a cherry on top."

Woof-woof.

"All right, I'll tell you why I won't," Isabel said. "Because every time we go for a joyride, you stick your head out the car window and howl at the bystanders on Main Street. It's embarrassing as all get out. I have to keep driving and pretending as if I don't see them pointing their fingers and grinning. Some of them are shooting a video of us with their smartphones to post online."

Woof-woof.

"You know the air conditioner is broken, and I have to leave the windows down, or else we'll roast inside the car."

Woof-woof.

"Don't be absurd. You can't stop doing it. All you hound dogs howl from moving cars. You just howl and howl like a canine banshee. It's not enough that your long ears flap in the wind. You have to be vocal about it, too."

Woof-woof.

Isabel chuckled. "Go ahead and be my guest. Bamboozle Alma into taking you. She's a wimp who indulges your every whim anyway."

"I could take Petey Samson," Alma said. "But he wants *you* to be the one who does it."

"Right, so the townies can guffaw and snort at me as we tootle by them," Isabel said. "I'm sick and tired of being the butt of their jokes."

"You're being paranoid," Alma said. "Pick up your stuff, and we'll blast off. Dinner won't be for another hour, so we have the time to see the sights around town."

Woof-woof.

"Oh, clam up the both of you," Isabel said. "It's Isabel's Reading Hour, and I've driven enough miles for one day."

Woof-woof.

"I agree, Petey Samson," Alma said. "Isabel is being a nincompoop. Let's sweeten the pot. We'll make the enticing offer of a fish and hush puppies dinner at Eddy's Deli if she agrees to chauffeur us."

"Impossible." Jutting her chin, Isabel put down the book and folded her arms on her chest. "I refuse to stoop so low as to accept a food bribe from my kid sister and our hound dog."

Woof-woof.

"He said he'll toss in a bear claw for dessert," Alma said.

"I'm not going deaf," Isabel said. "I heard what he said."

"Then what's it to be: do we or don't we go?" Alma asked.

"When am I supposed to read my detective novel?" Isabel replied.

"Read it when you should be sleeping, and then you can sleep after you die," Alma said.

"Now why didn't I think of doing that?" Isabel said.

◈ ◈ ◈

Sammi Jo rented in a snug apartment one floor above the town drugstore on Main Street. She liked its proximity to the town's goings-on that she could observe from her windows. Reynolds wasn't as fond of her digs as she was, but he'd slinked off to the Darlington Raceway. They were feuding about it over their smartphone connection.

"I know darn well I told you a couple of weeks ago about this big stock car race," Reynolds said. "Now didn't I, Sammi Jo?"

"You may have mumbled something or other about it," Sammi Jo replied. "You're always mumbling stuff, and I tune it out. But you didn't mark it on my wall calendar."

"It's your wall calendar, so you have an exclusive domain over it. Anyway, I called you to ask what's happening there."

"Well, since you've been gone, we've had a murder take place."

"The lurid news doesn't surprise me. Who is it?"

"Laura Isherwood died. Did you know her?"

"She was a hairstylist at Farrah's Beauty Shop and married to Deacon. I'm sorry to hear it because Laura was a friendly, caring person. How is Deacon taking it?"

"He's flaked out on his couch watching TV while taking advantage of his paid bereavement leave."

"Yeah, that sounds like the Deacon I know. What's his alibi? Does he have one to offer?"

"He claims he was on his way to work yesterday morning when Laura's killer struck. Would he murder her in the beauty shop?"

"Deacon packs a hot temper and flies off the handle easily. Would he get so angry he'd kill her? Offhand, I'd say probably not, but who knows? If you provoke him enough, he might lash out. If you said he killed her, I wouldn't disbelieve you."

"I've never had any personal dealings with him, so I don't know him as well as you do."

"Hey, don't get me wrong. Deacon Isherwood is no friend of mine, and I'd never sit down to have a beer with him."

"I don't like him based on what you and others have told me. We'll have to check him out."

"So, you still have some detective work to keep you busy until I return home."

"Thanks for the reminder, Reynolds, but I can think for myself."

"I wish you happy hunting and good luck. Well, I have to go see my buddy about a four-barrel carburetor, so I'll talk to you later. Stay safe and keep in touch."

"Cool your jets, Richard Petty. We ain't done talking, not by a long shot."

"What else is on your mind, sweet cheeks?"

"Don't play cute and coy with me. You know full well what's on my mind since it should be on your mind, too."

"Do I get three guesses to name it?"

"We have some unfinished business that needs attending to when you show your face here."

Reynolds forced a chuckle. "I've been thinking maybe we can work out a compromise for our wedding day."

"Okay, what is it?"

"What if we do a quickie, no-frills civil ceremony? Isabel and Alma can attend it along with your Aunt Phyllis if you like. I'll even remove my gimme hat and cover up my tiger head sleeve tattoos."

"What about my inviting Tabitha at the diner and the Three Musketeers?"

"I believe we can also accommodate them except the Three Musketeers can't have on their tie-dye t-shirts."

"Of course I'll want Eustis to be present."

"Why? He'll just bring his bag of pills."

"Because I said so. Dwight Holden will also receive an invitation."

"Why do you need a lawyer? We're just getting married."

"Dwight is my friend. Petey Samson will be in attendance, too."

"Nope. I'm drawing the line when it comes to having a flea-bitten hound dog at our wedding."

"What happened to your compromise, Reynolds?"

"Fine, he's in then. What do you say?"

"I say the chances it will come to pass are slim to nil, and Slim is lying in a morgue drawer."

"Boom. My best wedding idea just crashed and burned."

"When you return home, we're holding a come to Sammi Jo meeting. Do I have to spell out what I'm talking about?"

"I'm worldly enough to take your meaning."

"Of course you are, and that's why I love you. Now it's your turn. Have at it. I'm listening."

Reynolds coughed, cleared his throat, and coughed again.

"What's the matter? Have you caught a case of whooping cough?"

"You know I'm in the pink of health."

"Then you still owe me one. Go ahead."

"Yeah, yeah, I love you right back. How does that sound?"

"I reckon it'll have to do for the time being."

"Then I'll see you in a day or so," Reynolds said.

"Just come prepared to talk or don't bother to come at all," Sammi Jo said. "You can curl up and sleep with your precious four-barrel carburetor. Hubba-hubba, eh?"

Chapter 11

Sammi Jo had made a few modifications to her apartment.
Since the plank floor was a hideous dark wood, she'd covered it with
a beige carpet remnant. She'd taken a closer look at the Venetian
blinds and cringed. They no longer suited her purposes. When she
asked Eustis if she could do a makeover, he gave her free rein to
make all the alterations she saw fit to convert the apartment into her
personal living space. He still had a few things to learn about being a
landlord.

While Sammi Jo didn't go ape, she came close to it. Isabel and
Alma gave Sammi Jo a gift certificate, and she used it to buy the full-
length rose-hued curtains to give her living room the illusion of
height and depth. Her new coffee table had a clear Lucite top, and
she bought the art deco coasters from a vendor discounting them on
the flea market's last day.

In typical Reynolds fashion, he'd wimped out on installing the
new deadbolt lock, so she did it. She was a carpenter's daughter and
had inherited her father's tool belt. Her Shaker dining room set
constructed of fruitwood cherry was her pride and joy. The ginger
jar lamps lighting the end tables were new.

Isabel and Alma dropped by Sammi Jo's apartment shortly
before dinnertime. They'd paid for the carryout order--deluxe
cheeseburgers with boardwalk fries, red potato salad, and dill
pickles--from Eddy's Deli. Sammi Jo couldn't beat having dinner
brought to her doorstep. Like any Southern hostess, she kept an
enormous glass pitcher of sweet iced tea chilling on the top fridge
shelf. She briefed them on the information Reynolds had provided
her about Deacon.

"If laidback Reynolds says he doesn't like Deacon, that's saying a
lot," Alma said between devouring her cheeseburger and boardwalk
fries.

"I think we should probe a little into Deacon's past," Isabel said.

"Say the word and I'll go with you back to his place," Sammi Jo
said.

"Our return might agitate him to do something rash and dangerous," Alma said.

"We should find a safer alternative then," Isabel said.

"Did you remember to pick up the ketchup packets for the boardwalk fries?" Sammi Jo asked.

"We never leave Eddy's Deli without the ketchup packets," Alma replied.

"Jodie Wright's recent past is also worth checking into," Isabel said.

"Since she lived in Richmond, we heard so little about her," Alma said. "What's the story behind her divorce from Bernie? Sammi Jo, where is your laptop? It's time to put Mr. Google to work."

"Alma, give us a chance to finish our dinner," Isabel replied. "Also, congratulations on remembering it's Google, and not giggle, goggle, or gaggle."

"I don't mind getting started." Sammi Jo opened her laptop, booted it up, and opened a Google session. She typed in "Bernie Wright" and "Richmond," as the search words. She went through the results and traced him to a blue-collar suburb of Richmond, Virginia.

He'd set up a basic commercial website for his tree surgeon business. Upon examining the website, Sammi Jo noticed it hadn't been updated in several months. However, it provided an email address. She composed a brief message introducing herself with an explanation of what she wished to know and sent it.

"With any luck, Bernie will read my email and respond quickly," Sammi Jo said. "Or if it's a defunct email account, it will bounce like a rubber ball."

"Our first lead depends on getting a response, so let's hope it isn't the rubber ball kind of email," Isabel said.

"I love what you've done with your apartment," Alma said as she admired their surroundings.

"Thank you, Alma," Sammi Jo said. "Reynolds didn't notice any of the changes I made."

"Men." Alma laughed. "Where did you buy your ginger jar lamps?"

"Everything you see I either bought on sale at Target or from the local flea market vendors," Sammi Jo replied.

"You have an eye for spotting quality pieces," Isabel said. "The art deco coasters are a delight."

"We also scour the flea markets looking for our mysteries," Alma said. "You'd be amazed at what books the folks sell."

"How many books does a person need?" Sammi Jo asked. "You've already filled a large room with shelved books from the floor to the ceiling."

"Asking bookworms like us how many books are enough is like asking a surfer dude how many waves are enough," Alma replied.

"How many books do Isabel and you read?" Sammi Jo asked.

"Oh, it varies from week to week," Alma replied. "During a murder case like this one, our rate slows down. My current bookmark is tucked in a book I started two nights ago."

"How many books are your bookmarks tucked into, Isabel?" Sammi Jo asked.

"As of last night, I counted six of them," Isabel replied.

"How on earth can you read six books all at the same time?" Sammi Jo asked.

"I like to switch around while I'm reading them," Isabel replied. "Variety is the spice of life and all that neat stuff."

"How can you keep the different plots and main characters straight in your head?" Sammi Jo asked.

"I've never had a problem with it," Isabel replied. "Maybe I have a photographic memory that's able to compartmentalize the different stories."

Sammi Jo glanced over at Alma.

"Isabel is a virtual reading machine," Alma said. "I can't explain it, and I know I certainly can't do it."

"No wonder you have to hunt down so many books to keep you stocked up," Sammi Jo said.

"Thank goodness the supply of books never ends," Alma said.

"Have we received an email response yet?" Isabel asked.

Sammi Jo checked the laptop screen. "We sure have."

"Don't keep us waiting in suspense," Isabel said. "Open it and read it to us."

"The dreaded rubber ball email came back," Sammi Jo said. "My email sent to Bernie Wright bounced."

"We've run smack dab into another brick wall," Alma said.

"I can perform a few other Google searches," Sammi Jo said.

"Let's give Mr. Google a rest," Isabel said. "We've done so much sleuthing today I've worn holes in the soles of my gumshoes."

"The evening is still early," Alma said. "Stick a piece of cardboard inside your gumshoe, and we'll be off again."

"I'll resend my email to Bernie Wright," Sammi Jo said. "Maybe my second try will reach him."

"Would a Richmond trip to meet with Bernie be a profitable undertaking?" Isabel asked.

"Who'll babysit Petey Samson?" Alma replied.

"He'll travel with us," Isabel said. "Sammi Jo will go online and book our reservations to stay at a pet-friendly hotel."

"Just say when you're ready to go," Sammi Jo said.

"Petey Samson will poke his head out the car window and howl until we reach the Richmond city limits," Alma said.

"Then we'll put off taking our Richmond trip until I figure out a quieter way to get there," Isabel said.

∽ ∽ ∽

Isabel and Sheriff Fox conversed on their smartphones. Alma was driving since Isabel refused to do it and use her smartphone at the same time. She was a big believer in the better-safe-than-sorry rule.

"How goes the battle, Isabel?" Sheriff Fox asked.

"Fair to middling," Isabel replied. "How goes the playing computer Solitaire?"

"Fair to middling," Sheriff Fox replied without thinking. "I mean I don't play computer Solitaire at a critical time like this. What a ridiculous question you ask me."

"Roscoe, don't try to snow me," Isabel said. "I've known you since you were old enough to crawl around and shake a baby rattle."

"You didn't call up to give me a lecture," Sheriff Fox said.

"We're getting desperate to find a clue," Isabel said. "When has the M.E. scheduled Laura's autopsy?"

"The M.E. is on maternity leave," Sheriff Fox replied.

"Be that as it may, things shouldn't come to a screeching halt just because she's out having her baby. Aren't there other M.E.s, one of whom can fill in for her?"

"The substitution takes me a while to line up. Next week at this time we should have the autopsy results."

"Things have to proceed at a faster clip. I want to put this murder case to bed. It's cutting into my reading time, and it can't drag on for too much longer."

"Then you and Alma had better get cracking on it."

Sighing, Isabel lifted her eyes to the car's headliner.

"Is Roscoe perturbing you again?" Alma asked in a low voice.

Isabel nodded.

"I finally got a free moment to drive out to the Isherwoods' cottage and talk to Deacon," Sheriff Fox said.

"So...?" Isabel said.

"So as you can well imagine, Deacon is pretty shaken up about what happened to Laura. They married right out of high school and were inseparable. With one look at them, you could tell how much they loved each other."

"We also spoke to Deacon and left with just the opposite reaction. He seems largely indifferent to his wife's murder. He's more interested in enjoying his three days of paid bereavement leave than setting his affairs in order. He's turned into a couch potato while watching TV."

Sheriff Fox had a patronizing chuckle. "Isabel, Isabel, you surprise me. Here I thought a lady of your maturity and sophistication would know better. Haven't you learned anything about us males?"

Isabel felt a prick of irritation. "I expect I've learned a few things over the years about what makes you men tick. What are you referring to?"

"When we speak man to man as Deacon and I did, our conversations are more candid and articulate." Sheriff Fox repeated the patronizing chuckle. "We men know how to communicate with each other on a higher intellectual level than we do with you ladies. In other words, we men speak each other's lingo."

"Will you pardon me for one moment, Roscoe?"

"Why, certainly, Isabel. Is there anything wrong?"

"Alma and I have to strap on our life vests. It's piling up that fast and furious, and we don't want to drown in it."

"If you listen closely, you'll notice I'm not laughing."

"I suppose the next thing you'll tell me is Deacon had no reason to murder Laura, and he's innocent as a newborn baby."

"Exactly, so we'll have to agree to disagree on making him a murder suspect."

"That's fine. Just don't stand in our way as we check him out. He's not our prime suspect, but we have our eyes on him. By the way, who's your prime suspect?"

"I'm not disclosing that privileged information over the air."

"Why not? We've discussed all of your other privileged information."

"Suffice it to say, I'm still collecting evidence and can't tell you what I've found."

Isabel had to laugh. "Oh please, stop pulling my leg. I don't see you suddenly turning energetic and disciplined enough to go out and gather evidence."

"My colleagues in the Virginia Sheriffs Association don't call me Roscoe the Bloodhound for nothing."

"Do they call you this after they've hit the open bar?"

"I have to go, Isabel. Abigail just returned to the office."

"Enjoy your fresh batch of doughnuts. Bye for now."

Isabel was so disgusted she felt the urge to toss her smartphone out the car window except for Sheriff Fox, not her smartphone, was the source of her vexation.

"Don't let it get to you, Isabel. We'll double down on our efforts and discover who Laura's killer is," Alma said.

"We're already working on it as fast as we can go. Women our ages don't have an overdrive gear to engage."

"Then we'll bank on catching a lucky break. Every now and then we stumble upon one of those."

"We do on occasion catch one. Be sure to rub your rabbit's foot, and I'll carry my lucky horseshoe and my four-leaf clover."

Alma laughed. "With all that good luck going for us, how can we lose?"

"Home, James, and don't spare the horses. I've finished my sleuthing activities for today, and it's time to rest up for tomorrow's battles."

"I'll break out the brown jug for our nightcap," Alma said. "I'm thinking two or three snorts should have us falling asleep as soon as our heads hit the pillows. How does that sound to you?"

"Bottoms up," Isabel replied.

Chapter 12

The next morning Isabel stood at the picture window blowing on the steamy cup of coffee she held. She wore a powder blue housecoat as well as an irked scowl in reaction to what she observed across the street. Their lazy neighbor hadn't mowed his grass in so long he appeared to be growing a yardful of barley or wheat. She wondered if he had a different concept of what a mowed lawn was than she did.

Isabel considered buying him a herd of billy goats to keep his lawn trimmed, except they'd probably wander over to munch on their morning newspaper, wash line laundry, and prized zinnias. She had an urge to pop over and raise a holy stink, but she wasn't the confrontational type. Instead, she'd get the impetuous Alma to take up the prickly issue with him. Isabel finished her cup of coffee and left to get dressed.

They made their weekly excursion to the farmers' market held in the municipal parking lot near the railroad tracks. The farmers' market kept them supplied with fresh produce. Since the sunny morning had low humidity, the sisters put on their walking shoes, found their reusable tote bags, and struck out for the farmers' market.

"You've had another night to sleep on our murder mystery. What are your latest thoughts?" Isabel asked.

"I'm leaning toward Deacon as the one who did it," Alma replied.

"You sound pretty sure of it. Tell me why."

"Despite his claims of their undying love and affection, the Isherwoods must've had a nasty quarrel, and Laura didn't go with him to his company picnic. Phyllis told us she saw them bickering in the bank parking lot. Laura never talked about her marriage while she styled our hair. Moreover, he didn't act much like a grieving husband during our visit with him. Now you can give me your two cents."

"I'm like you in finding Deacon guilty for the reasons you gave. However, I'm not willing to dismiss Jodie. Something about her rubs me the wrong way, and, as you know, I'm fairly easy to get along with, so I'm listening to my hunch."

Alma was disappointed. "I haven't formed a decent hunch in so long, I've forgotten how one feels. I'm afraid I'm all hunched out. Can it happen to us older women? Is it inevitable as getting varicose veins and liver spots?"

"I'm confident you'll form a new hunch very soon."

"I look forward to it. There's nothing more satisfying than forming a hunch."

Isabel's smartphone ringtone was a Charlie Parker saxophone riff. She checked the caller ID and made a face like she'd done while abhorring their lazy neighbor's jungle lawn.

"Who is it?" Alma asked.

"The worst possible caller you can imagine," Isabel replied.

"You may as well get it over with. If you ignore him, you know he won't go away or give up on trying to contact you."

Isabel reluctantly followed Alma's advice, put on the speakerphone, and exchanged greetings with Sheriff Fox.

"I'm reporting a significant development on the Laura Isherwood homicide," Sheriff Fox said. "I'm set to leave here and go arrest Farrah Patel for it."

"You're as predictable as today's sunrise," Isabel said. "You always single out the easiest murder suspect to arrest."

"Color me boring, predictable, or whatever you wish, but I'm ready to close the book on it. You and Alma can return to your soap operas, iced teas, and hound dog. Your meddling services are no longer required."

"Skip the sarcasm."

"Sarcasm has nothing to do with it. I'm issuing you a direct order to cease and desist your sleuthing activities. Your town sheriff has spoken, and you'd do well to heed his instructions."

"Nope."

"I beg your pardon, Isabel? What did you just say?"

"Have you got an earwax blockage? I said nope, spelled N-O-P-E."

"I thought that's what I heard, but I wanted to be sure I wasn't hearing things."

"Alma and I are defying your direct order and proceeding as if we never held this phone conversation. So there you go, Sheriff Fox. Deal with it as you see fit, and see if I give a flying fig."

Alma wasn't as certain. "Maybe we should give his direct order a little thought, Isabel. The poor lighting in the prison cells causes eyestrain while the inmates read their books. Plus, the prison warden prohibits taking in pets like Petey Samson. And those prison shoes. Lord-a-mercy, have you taken a close look at their butt-ugly footwear?"

"Is that Alma I can hear speaking?" Sheriff Fox asked.

"Don't get your hopes up," Isabel replied. "Alma backs me to the hilt on my decisions. We Trumbo sisters stick together through thick and thin."

"Of course the exception is always possible," Alma said.

Isabel fixed her get-on-board-with-me-now-sis stare on Alma.

"You're being obstinate and contrary on purpose," Sheriff Fox said.

"I'm striving to find the truth behind Laura's murder," Isabel said. "If it makes me obstinate and contrary, then so be it."

"What does it take to convince you Farrah is Laura's killer?" Sheriff Fox asked.

"We'd like to see the physical evidence proving it," Isabel replied. "For instance, have you recovered the murder weapon?"

"As of yet, it hasn't come to light," Sheriff Fox replied. "However, I fully expect to lay my hands on it before long."

"Your explanation won't satisfy a jury to convict Farrah," Isabel said. "Know what I mean?"

"All right, I'll give you twenty-four hours and not a minute longer," Sheriff Fox said. "If you find who you think Laura's killer is, then be sure *you* have the physical evidence to back it up."

"Something significant just occurred to me," Isabel said.

"Don't be shy about sharing it," Sheriff Fox said.

"I can discern how a disturbing pattern about us has developed," Isabel said. "You rush to arrest the easiest suspect, the low-hanging fruit, on each murder case because you know it spurs Alma and me to bear down and identify the actual killer. Now isn't my insight the gospel truth?"

"No comment," Sheriff Fox replied.

"Roscoe, you're a manipulative, devious law enforcement officer and a scoundrel to boot," Isabel said. "And those, sir, are your good qualities."

"Stick and stones, Isabel, but I get results," Sheriff Fox said. "The town voters expect it, and they reelect me because I deliver the goods."

"You deliver the goods only because Alma and I give them to you," Isabel said.

"Again, no comment," Sheriff Fox said. "Will that be all? I'm a little busy winding up a murder case."

Too disgusted to continue their conversation, Isabel hung up in his ear, not as emphatic as slamming down the phone receiver had sounded back in the good old days.

"We'll get back to our sleuthing right after we return home from the farmers' market," Alma said.

"I say horsefeathers on the farmers' market." Isabel spun around and headed back home. "The zucchini and squash can wait, but our sleuthing sure can't."

"But I like adding the sliced up zucchini and squash to my toss salads."

"Our sleuthing comes first," Isabel said. "Sheriff Fox is using Farrah's arrest as the way to coerce us to work harder and present him with the real solution."

"The man has demonstrated time and again he lacks any scruples," Alma said. "He'll pull any underhanded trick he can think of to come out smelling like a rose."

"I'll sic Petey Samson on him," Isabel said.

Isabel and Alma approached their brick rambler where she spotted who waited on the front porch. She scrunched her eyes as she spoke.

"Uh-oh, we've got some company," Alma said.

"Poor Harriet looks as if she's blown a main gasket," Isabel said.

"Are we expected to fix it?" Alma asked.

"We have the reputation for being the town's fixers," Isabel replied.

"Then I propose we change our reputation," Alma said.

"It's too late for doing that now," Isabel said.

They waved at Harriet arising from the front porch step and striding up the concrete walkway. Tall and angular, she'd a narrow face with an aquiline nose, thin lips, and almond-shaped eyes. Her tomato red batik sundress had half-sleeves, and she wore chunky sandals. Before Isabel could invite her inside to the living room, she was wagging her finger and barking at them.

"Have you heard the disturbing rumor? Well, have you?" Harriet fumed. "Farrah Patel won't be doing my weekly touch-ups if she's arrested by Sheriff Fox. What am I supposed to do then? Can you tell me? Will I have to drive to Warrenton to find a hairstylist?"

"It's still just a rumor, Harriet," Isabel replied. "Nothing bad has occurred yet. Calm down a little and get a grip."

"But what if Farrah is arrested? Take a look at my blah hair." Harriet lowered her head for them to see. "When I peered in the vanity mirror this morning, do you know what I did? Well, I'll tell you. I nearly went psycho. My hair is a birds' nest of tangles, snarls, and knots. I can't do anything with it, and I need a professional to tame it."

"What do you expect from us?" Alma asked. "We have no hair-taming expertise."

"You're the only troubleshooters I know," Harriet replied. "You have the knack to set things right so get busy and stop Farrah's arrest."

"You vastly overrate our abilities," Isabel said.

"At least you can attempt to do something," Harriet said. "I've been getting through not just a bad hair day but bad hair *week*."

"Have you thought of wearing a lampshade or perhaps a Chewbacca mask?" Alma replied.

Harriet furrowed her brow. "Huh?"

"Alma, be nice," Isabel said. "Harriet, your hairdo looks flattering as it is. Take it from me. Nobody will say anything. Right, Alma?"

"I'd better plead the Fifth," Alma replied.

"Sheriff Fox is wrong as wrong can be," Harriet said. "Farrah is no more a killer than you or me. She cuts hair. That's it. But she sure as sugar can't cut hair if she's languishing behind bars."

"A murder took place in her beauty shop," Isabel said. "An evil person killed Laura, and Sheriff Fox has the sworn duty to arrest who did it."

"He should forget about Farrah and investigate it more thoroughly." Harriet had a better handle on her roiled emotions and spoke in an even voice.

"We're also concerned since Laura was our hairstylist," Isabel said.

"I prefer to book my appointments with Farrah," Harriet said. "I had nothing against Laura, but I don't mind paying a few dollars more for the professional experience."

"Are you acquainted with Deacon Isherwood?" Isabel asked.

"Deacon has never done anything unkind to me, but I refuse to have any dealings with him," Harriet said.

"Did you see anybody who isn't a customer at the beauty shop?" Isabel asked.

Thinking back, Harriet tilted her face while she scratched her chin. She closed her eyes while Alma gave Isabel a dubious look. So far, they'd learned nothing of value from Harriet, and Alma was no longer hopeful they would.

Just then, a lawn mower sputtered to life. Isabel and Alma's heads snapped around like wind socks to gaze across the street. Their lazy neighbor had deigned to come out of the house, power up the lawn mower, and cut the tall grass. Hearing the small engine's rumble was a cause for exchanging celebratory high fives. When he waved his hand at them, Isabel wanted to wave something else-- there's a first time for everything--back at him, but she just returned his gesture. Seeing they were talking, he moved away to mow the backyard first with the noisy lawn mower.

"The last time I arrived early for my hair appointment," Harriet said. "I had a seat and fiddled with my smartphone until I saw Tallulah Pettigrew open the door. Tapping her titanium cane, she doddered up to Laura, and they went into the break room for a closed-door meeting. Laura soon returned to her styling station and resumed her work. She muttered a perfunctory apology to her customer for the delay."

"Did Farrah disapprove of Laura's interruption?" Isabel asked.

"I saw Farrah give Laura a stern look," Harriet replied. "I'm fairly certain after the customers left, Farrah took Laura aside for a word. Farrah runs a tight ship and protects her brand."

"She's a no-nonsense businesswoman," Isabel said. "I guess she has no other choice if she wants to make a successful go of her beauty shop."

"I admire her self-discipline," Harriet said. "She eats healthy, doesn't smoke or drink, and works out regularly."

"How utterly boring," Alma said.

Isabel gave Alma one of her big sister frowns.

"Is she into yoga, Zumba, or Pilates?" Isabel asked.

"Actually, she told me she likes to exercise with Indian clubs at home," Harriet replied. "Are you familiar with them?"

"I've seen the photos of Indian clubs," Isabel replied. "I didn't realize folks still use them as exercise equipment."

"Falling into the wrong hands, they sound dangerous," Alma said.

"You have to know what you're doing while you're using them," Isabel said.

"I've never heard of an Indian club instructor," Alma said.

"Then Farrah learned from the instructions given on a website," Isabel said.

"What private business did Tallulah and Laura have to conduct behind closed doors?" Alma asked.

"I can hazard an educated guess," Isabel said. "We know Tallulah is a smart cookie who saved her nickels and dimes over the years. She owns and rents several townhouses."

"Was Laura inquiring about the availability of one?" Alma asked. "Was she getting her ducks in a row to leave Deacon?"

"She had a full-time job with benefits, earned good tips, and could swing making the rent," Isabel replied.

"Will Tallulah share what she knows?" Alma asked.

"There's only one way to find out," Isabel replied. "We'll have to ask her."

"Are you feeling any calmer and steadier now, Harriet?" Alma asked.

"I feel much better, thank you. Our talking about it has lessened my anxiety," Harriet replied. "I flew into a hysterical panic when I first heard Farrah might be arrested and tossed into jail."

"Where did you hear the rumor?" Isabel asked.

"Deputy Sheriff Bexley told me it would happen soon," Harriet replied.

"Next time you should consider the source of the rumor," Isabel said. "Deputy Sheriff Bexley isn't the most reliable person to trust for getting accurate information."

Chapter 13

The day had warmed up to incite the cicadas--some folks called them heat bugs--to sing at a high-pitched din in the trees. Alma led them into the yard and up the flagstone path, passing by the satellite dish painted flat green and half-hidden in the purple fountain grass. Sammi Jo brought up the rear with Petey Samson on his leash. Fortunately, Tallulah Pettigrew sat out on the front porch. She spoke in a quavery country drawl as they reached the bottom porch step.

"To what do I owe the honor of this visit, ladies?" Tallulah asked.

Isabel rested for a brief moment while she took measure of Tallulah in the Adirondack chair. Her titanium cane leaned against it. A cat's-paw breeze wafted through the shady porch, creating a choice spot to relax and savor the summer morning. The brass wind chimes tinkled, while the hanging pots of geraniums and petunias swayed. The half-full glass pitcher of lemonade sweated on the spindle table beside her.

"We come wearing our sleuth hats," Isabel replied. "Even Petey Samson has on his little sleuth hat. See it?"

Tallulah had a pleasant laugh. "Why don't you come in out of the hot sun and rest your feet for a spell? Share an ice-cold glass of lemonade with me, and we'll chat."

Without a word, Alma stepped forward to mount the porch steps, but Isabel reached out, snagged Alma's sleeve, and detained her. She tugged her arm to detach it, but Isabel held on tighter.

"Thanks for your kind hospitality," Isabel said. "However, we're in a hurry, so another time would be better."

The miffed Alma finally yanked her sleeve free from Isabel's grasp. "Speak for yourself since I'm in no hurry," Alma said.

"You're always my honored guests," Tallulah said. "What brings you by?"

"You've probably heard about our role in the investigation of Laura Isherwood's murder," Isabel replied.

"It's general knowledge what you're doing," Tallulah said.

"We need to know what you discussed with her in the break room at the beauty shop," Isabel said.

"I promised Laura I'd have a townhouse ready, and I'd get back to her as soon as I could, so I met with her at work," Tallulah replied.

"Farrah wasn't pleased you kept Laura from styling her customer's hair," Isabel said.

"I'm nearly eighty-one and totter around on a titanium hip, so I'm not worried about what the folks think of me," Tallulah said.

Isabel nodded. "I take your point. Did Laura say why she wanted to rent the townhouse?"

"She didn't tell me, and I didn't think it was my place to ask her," Tallulah replied. "She needed a place to rent, and I needed to rent a place, so we struck a business deal. That settled that."

"Laura must've formed a plan to move out on Deacon," Isabel said.

"I came to pretty much the same conclusion," Tallulah said.

"Was she keeping it a secret until she was ready to do it?" Isabel asked.

"She asked me not to say anything to anybody," Tallulah replied. "But I wouldn't have anyway. Unlike many of the townies, I avoid gossip like the plague."

Somehow, Alma had the willpower not to scoff or smirk.

"Had Laura settled on a moving date?" Isabel asked.

"I told her I didn't like my townhouse to sit unoccupied, and she said she'd be moved into it within a week," Tallulah replied. "Her assurance satisfied me, and I dropped the matter."

"Had she been bringing her belongings to leave them at the townhouse?" Isabel asked.

"I gave her the door key after she paid me the first month's rent and security deposit," Tallulah replied. "I never saw or spoke to her again."

"Surely, she brought up Deacon and their marital squabbles," Alma said.

"We both knew why she wanted to rent the townhouse, and I saw no reason to discuss it to embarrass or shame her," Tallulah said.

"Did you give her a break on the rent?" Isabel asked.

"It's my business if I reduced her rent," Tallulah replied. "I liked her, and I felt sorry for her over what she was going through with Deacon."

"Have you had any contact with him?" Isabel asked.

"Fortunately, I've never had any reason to see the man," Tallulah replied. "I'd like to keep it that way."

"He's not a likable individual or a dazzling conversationalist," Isabel said.

"Laura deserved better for a husband, and she was taking the necessary steps to correct her mistake," Tallulah said.

"Did she tell you her marriage was a mistake?" Isabel asked.

"Not in so many words but I could tell by the regretful inflection of her voice what their story was." Tallulah took a long sip of lemonade from the tall glass and wiped off her lips on a tissue. "I'm plum tuckered out, Isabel. Have we touched on everything you wanted to speak to me about?"

Isabel glanced at Alma who gave a slight nod. "You've been a help," Isabel said. "Thank you for giving us your time."

"You're most welcome, and no thanks are needed," Tallulah said. "If I can play a small part in the apprehension of Laura's killer, I'll feel blessed."

"Have you got an extra door key to your townhouse?" Alma asked. "We'd like to get started as soon as we can."

"You may take my door key and search for the clues as much as you like." Arising, Tallulah reached for her titanium cane. "The sooner we can put this bloody business behind us, the better off we'll be."

"You'd better believe it," Alma said. "By the way, are you going to drink the rest of your lemonade? I'd hate for it to spoil."

"Come along, Alma," Isabel said. "We already told Tallulah our goodbyes."

"Why are you always in such a hurry?" Alma asked.

"You don't need any lemonade," Isabel replied.

◈ ◈ ◈

"Ossie, what's the latest and greatest news, my good man?" Blue asked his fellow bench dweller.

Turning his head, Ossie spat on the sidewalk. "Oh, you know, it's the same old same old."

"Same stuff on a different day sums it up," Blue said.

"Yep." Ossie nodded. "You pretty much nailed it on the head."

"Have you heard any recent tidings from your sweet amour?" Blue asked.

"Alas, for Isabel Trumbo remains just my platonic friend and not my sweet amour," Ossie replied. "Much to my chagrin, I hasten to add. My heart is broken, and it may never mend. I'm doomed to pine away for her until I draw my final breath."

"Keep your chin up and don't succumb to the lovesick blues," Willie said. "Who among us understands the fickle ways of romance? Look at it this way. If Romeo and Juliet couldn't get it sorted out, then I'd say nobody ever will."

"You realize Romeo and Juliet are the figments of Billy Shakespeare's imagination," Blue said.

"Of course I know it," Willie said. "I'm employing poetic license to illustrate a point for Ossie's benefit."

"Not to belabor the topic, but your point is lost on me," Blue said.

"Blue, go take a long walk on a short pier," Willie said. "Do you get my point now?"

Blue grunted.

"Anyway, I've asked Isabel to be my wife so many times my head is left in a spin," Ossie said. "She keeps rebuffing my heartfelt overtures, and I don't know if I've worn her down one bit."

Willie nodded. "You are a persistent bugger. I'll give you credit for that much."

"Could she be playing hard to get?" Blue said. "I'm not the world's foremost judge of women, but I have it on good authority they can play coy and cagey sometimes."

Ossie brightened up. "Do you think so, Blue?"

"My notion is that mature women like Isabel don't lose their feminine mushiness and sentimentality," Blue said. "They still prefer their male suitors to come around and pitch them woo."

"Pitch them woo?" Ossie looked dumbstruck. "What is a woo, and how do I pitch it? Overhand, sidearm, or underhand?"

"You know, flatter them by bringing them bouquets of long-stemmed red roses and boxes of Belgian chocolates," Blue replied. "Just make sure the red roses don't have aphids, and the Belgian chocolates don't exceed their sell-by date."

"If that's true, then I still may have a shot at winning Isabel's heart," Ossie said. "Blue, you're a genius."

"Thanks for the shout-out, but I already know it," Blue said.

"I don't mean to rain on your parade, Genius," Willie said. "But I contend Isabel has made up her mind for keeps. She's finished with the marriage track. One and done is plenty enough for her."

"Well sir, I like Blue's take more than yours, so I'm sticking with him," Ossie said. "I'm taking one more shot at sweeping Isabel off her feet. Who knows? Maybe this time will be the charm, and she'll agree to be Mrs. Conger."

"Hope springs eternal as the poet says," Blue said. "Of course you'll have to remember to always leave the toilet seat down."

"Say again?" Ossie asked.

"Never mind," Blue said. "She'll let you know if the time ever comes up."

"Picture it, fellows. I'll have my wife at home to cook, clean, and shop for me again." Ossie beamed. "I'll be back in hog heaven."

"Um, Ossie, you might want to rethink your reasons for remarrying," Willie said.

"Oh yeah? Why is that?" Ossie asked.

"Today's wives don't cook, clean, and shop for their husbands anymore," Willie replied.

Ossie was flabbergasted. "Then why do today's women get married?"

"Well, you see, marriage is considered an equal partnership where the husband carries more of the load than we did back in our glory days," Willie replied. "Don't you ever tune in and watch Dr. Phil's TV show?"

"Who is Dr. Phil?" Ossie replied.

"Holy gee, I give up, Ossie," Willie said, throwing up his hands. "You're a hopeless case."

"At any rate, I take it neither of you has any news on how their sleuthing goes," Blue said.

"No update has reached me," Ossie said. "I like to go by the rule stipulating no news is good news."

"We might be getting a phone call from them anytime now with the triumphant news they've solved it," Willie said.

"Yeah boy, the Trumbo sisters know their sleuthing stuff like nobody's business," Blue said. "It's lights out when they take on a new murder mystery."

"They're smart as a pair of hoot owls," Willie said.

"All right, guys, let's dial it back on the praise," Ossie said. "I'm already broken-hearted enough as it is without you telling me how fabulous Isabel is, and I can't take her for my wife."

"Ossie, you're acting like a lovelorn teenager whose girl crush turned him down for a date," Blue said.

"I just can't help it," Ossie said.

"You should join forces with Sammi Jo," Willie said. "She's trying to get married to Reynolds like you are to Isabel. You could swap romance tips and plot your strategies."

"What makes you think we haven't already done so?" Ossie asked.

"All I can tell you is hang in there," Blue said.

"I'm not sure how much longer I have to hang in there," Ossie said.

"Bear in mind age is just a number in your head," Willie said.

"My problem is the number keeps going up," Ossie said.

A whipcord lean six-footer with an oily smirk stepped out of the Azul Lago Florist Shop and regarded the Three Musketeers seated on the wooden bench. Stopping, he nodded at them.

"Good morning, Deacon," Willie said. "We're sorry for your loss. Laura was a mighty fine woman. I can't tell you how dearly we'll miss her."

"I appreciate your thoughtful concern and kind words," Deacon said. "I just placed an order of lilies and roses for her funeral whenever her autopsy is completed."

"Laura's funeral gives everybody the opportunity to gather together and grieve properly for her loss," Willie said. "The townies will come to it and pay their respects."

"We buried our late wives that way," Ossie said.

"You three fellows are widowers," Deacon said. "I did not know that."

"Fact is, we've been widowers for longer than we care to remember," Willie said.

"We're destined to die as widowers," Ossie said. "No matter how hard we struggle to remarry, it's not in the cards for at least one of the Three Musketeers. Let me tell you what, it's a brutal, cold world out there."

"Ossie, please get over yourself," Blue said.

"It's a lot easier said than done," Ossie said.

"Have you seen Isabel and Alma lately?" Deacon asked.

Willie narrowed his eyes, a shrewd glint in them. "Why might you ask us?"

Deacon shrugged. "They drove out to the house with Blaine and talked to me. I'm curious as to what they're doing now."

"We haven't spoken to them since you probably last did," Willie said.

"Laura was their hairstylist, and they're upset she's gone," Deacon said.

"Her murder upsets lots of the townies," Willie said. "We're counted in their number, too."

"I'm finding it out more and more." Deacon rubbed the back of his neck. "Laura knew half of the town, it seems. I guess she met them while she cut their hair. We didn't talk shop all that much at the dinner table."

"Speaking of jobs, why aren't you at yours?" Willie asked. "Did you get fired?"

"Mr. Dunfee put me on paid bereavement leave," Deacon replied. "Aren't Isabel and Alma like private detectives?"

"They prefer to go by the label amateur sleuths," Willie replied.

"Amateur sleuths, eh?" Deacon did the neck-rubbing gesture again. "How do you like that? I've never heard of such a thing." He gazed across Main Street before he peered down at Willie. "What might the amateur sleuths like them do?"

"You'd have to ask them how they do their sleuthwork," Willie replied.

"They were born inquisitive, so it comes as natural as breathing to them," Blue said.

"Is it their hobby they do in their spare time?" Deacon asked.

"I'd say it's more like their obsession they do all the time," Ossie replied.

"Oh yeah, I give that a big definite," Blue said.

"But don't you worry about a thing, Deacon," Willie said. "They'll be thorough, and they'll track down the party responsible for Laura's murder. Their track record is second to none."

Smiling, Deacon nodded. "Nobody wants to see Laura's killer arrested more than me. I'm surprised Sheriff Fox hasn't already taken her killer into custody, and I can't wait until he does."

"We can understand your wanting to see that justice is carried out," Blue said.

"Isabel and Alma will probably come to see you again," Willie said. "So, they'll find you before you can find them."

"They do get around for seniors, don't they?" Deacon said.

"You can't keep the dynamic sister duo tied down," Willie said.

"Yeah, yeah, tell me about it," the dejected Ossie said.

Smiling, Blue rubbed his finger over his thumb. "Can you hear me, Ossie? I'm playing a heartbreaking tune on the world's tiniest violin just for you."

"Blue, eat my shorts," Ossie said.

Willie chuckled at them.

"I've got a few things to look after before the day is done," Deacon said. "You fellows take it easy."

"You do likewise, young man," Willie said.

"Don't squat on your spurs," Ossie said.

After Deacon paused to let a farm tractor and hay wagon pass by, he crossed Main Street.

Willie made an observation. "Methinks Deacon walks with the swagger of a man getting away with bloody murder."

"Oh yeah, I give that a big definite," Blue said.

"That just ain't right," Willie said.

"I'll call Isabel with the update of our interesting chat with him," Blue said.

"Be sure to tell her I said hello," Ossie said. "Also remind her I'm free on Friday and Saturday nights."

"She'll just laugh again and say what a kidder you are," Blue said.

"I'll show her what a kidder I am after I take a little blue pill." Ossie chortled under his breath. "The sly old dog Ossie will show her a thing or two about how he pitches woo like an All-Star."

Chapter 14

Tallulah had lent them her door key to the townhouse she'd rented to the late Laura Isherwood. The two designated parking slots were empty, and Isabel feared the townhouse would also be as empty and bereft of clues. The small front lawn was mowed, and the boxwood hedge trimmed. Isabel unlocked the townhouse door, raised all the windows, and the cross-breeze helped to air out the hot, stuffy rooms.

"Welcome to home sweet home," Alma said.

"We can do without the snarky comments," Isabel said.

"What can I tell you?" Alma said. "I'm just a snarky sleuth."

"Laura wouldn't have moved in here without first applying a dust rag, vacuum cleaner, and lots of Pine-Sol," Sammi Jo said.

"It depended on how desperate Laura was to get out of her troubled domestic situation," Isabel said.

Petey Samson sneezed.

"God bless you, sweetie pie," Isabel said.

"She always says that after he sneezes," Alma said.

"Decide on what comes next and let's get on with it," Isabel said.

"If Sheriff Fox beat us here, he found all the clues and left nothing for us," Sammi Jo said.

"Aw, phooey," Alma said. "Roscoe wouldn't know a clue, good or bad, if it were a snapping turtle and bit him on the end of his nightstick. Or wherever."

"Ouch," Isabel said.

"If I were Laura coming in for the first time, I'd make a beeline for the kitchen," Sammi Jo said. "I'd want the fridge and stove functioning before I took up residence."

"An operable microwave and freezer are also desirable amenities," Alma said.

Isabel thrust out her hand at Alma. "Break out the tools of our trade, and we'll get busy."

"Me?" Alma had an astonished expression. "It's not my turn to carry them."

Isabel's jaw dropped. "You're mistaken because I distinctly remember it was my turn on our last murder case."

"Well, I didn't stick our magnifying glasses in my pocketbook," Alma said. "We'll have to rely on our naked eye."

"How can we?" Isabel asked. "We're almost blind as a mole."

"I'll be the one who sees any clues we happen across," Sammi Jo said.

"So ordered," Isabel said.

"I'm going to rig up a fanny pack for Petey Samson to strap on," Alma said. "He'll transport our magnifying glasses inside it as a Saint Bernard does with the brandy in the rescue keg collar."

"Petey Samson is just our ace tracker dog," Isabel said.

"Sammi Jo, please take the lead if you will," Alma said. "Isabel is turning into a bossy-pants again, and she's pushing my buttons."

Isabel counted to three to refrain from rolling her eyes, but it was a futile effort.

The kitchen appeared less than clean, and Alma balked at the entrance until Isabel dragged her into it. Sputtering with indignation, Alma detached herself from Isabel's grasp.

"Will you quit grabbing me like a geriatric octopus?" Alma said.

"I'm shepherding you along as an elder sister would," Isabel said.

"I'm a big girl, so I don't require any shepherding," Alma said.

"Don't be so sure about that," Isabel said.

"Why don't you look in the fridge?" Alma asked.

Isabel cracked open the fridge door, leaned over to peer inside it, and shut it.

"Nothing," Isabel said. "Have a peek in the microwave."

"If the fridge is empty, then the microwave probably is, too," Alma said.

"What a nincompoop thing to say," Isabel said. "Check inside the microwave like I did the fridge."

"Why? What clue might lurk in there?" Alma asked.

"How the devil should I know?" Isabel replied. "Maybe Laura's killer left his or her business card for us."

"Ho-ho and yuk-yuk, Isabel," Alma said.

Alma checked out the microwave, electric range oven, and dishwasher. Meantime, Isabel opened the cupboards, and Sammi Jo rooted through the floor cabinets. They didn't find anything useful.

"Laura brought some flatware with a couple of pots and pans," Isabel said. "She was making a few early preparations to live here."

"Don't tell Tallulah I said it, but her townhouse would never make the front cover of *Architectural Digest*," Alma said.

"Laura took whatever she could find in her price range on short notice," Isabel said.

Crunch-crunch-crunch.

"No, Petey Samson!" Isabel looked aghast at him. "Don't eat the tortilla chip on the filthy kitchen floor! Oh, the horrid germs and the contagion! You'll get cholera! Or beriberi! Bad doggie! Bad! Bad!"

He froze in place with a corner of the tortilla chip sticking out of his mouth and rolled up his soulful brown eyes at her.

"Don't we feed you?" Isabel asked. "Jumpy charges us a pretty penny for the dog food he sells at his grocery market."

"Petey Samson is bored," Alma said. "I can identify with him."

"Give him a doggie treat, and he'll forget about snacking on the tortilla chip," Sammi Jo said.

"I forgot to bring the doggie treats," Isabel said. "Besides, he deserves no reward. He's a dud who hasn't picked up one promising scent. Some ace tracker dog he is."

Alma knelt by Petey Samson and patted him on the head as she spoke to him.

"Isabel says you're a dud for a doggie," Alma said. "But she's wrong and doesn't speak for me because I know you're the best doggie there ever was. Now, who's your mama?"

Petey Samson dropped the tortilla chip from his mouth and woofed-woofed at Alma. He licked her across the cheek and woofed-woofed again.

"You darn tootin' I am and don't you ever forget it, pooch," Alma said. "Regrettably, I also didn't bring any doggie treats." She held out her empty hands to demonstrate to him.

Petey Samson picked up the tortilla chip and chewed it again.

Isabel sighed. "We're spinning our wheels in here."

"The bedrooms upstairs await us," Sammi Jo said.

The townhouse upstairs consisted of three small bedrooms and a hall bath as well as the washer and dryer fitted into a hallway alcove to eliminate hauling the heavy laundry baskets up and down the two flights of stairs. In the sunniest, largest bedroom was an army cot with a folded-up pile of sheets and summer blankets lying on the end. The pillow looked fluffed up, and the alarm clock, a twin-bell, wind-up model, sat on an inverted milk crate serving as a night table.

"We see more evidence Laura was setting up to make a fresh start of things," Isabel said.

"What did she leave in the closet?" Alma asked.

Sammi Jo slid open the double closet doors and revealed the reach-in closet was also bare. "She hadn't gotten too far with her preparations."

"She'd pick a day when Deacon was away to move in most of her belongings," Isabel said.

"What happened when he got home and discovered she was gone?" Alma asked.

"Maybe she hadn't thought her plan through that far," Isabel replied.

"We've laid another goose egg to go with the others," Alma said. "Let's return Tallulah's door key with our thanks."

Sammi Jo slid the double closet doors shut and followed Alma out of the bedroom. However, Isabel remained behind.

"Aren't you coming with us?" Alma asked.

"I'm not ready to leave quite yet," Isabel replied.

"Now what is it with you?" Alma asked.

"We haven't turned over all the stones," Isabel replied.

"What stone is left unturned?" Alma asked.

"Name the one item Laura would have concealed if she knew she'd be living here soon," Isabel replied.

"Money?" Alma replied.

"She'd need cash to cover her living expenses until she got on her feet," Isabel said. "But try again, Alma."

"Why don't you just tell us what you're thinking instead of my guessing it?" Alma said.

"Laura was a quiet, introspective woman not given to discussing her personal affairs with anybody," Isabel replied.

"True enough," Alma said.

"Therefore she needed an outlet for expressing her emotions and feelings, and my hunch is she kept a daily journal or diary," Isabel said.

Alma regarded Sammi Jo. "What do you think?" she asked.

"Isabel's hunch makes sense to me," Sammi Jo replied.

"You wonder if Laura stashed her diary somewhere in here," Alma said. "Finding and reading it might point us to her killer."

"Taking a look at it might be the breakthrough clue we seek," Isabel said.

"She wouldn't store it at home because Deacon might stumble across it," Alma said.

"If he saw what she'd written about him, he'd blow his stack and attack her in revenge," Isabel said.

"Petey Samson, go find Laura's diary," Alma said. "Fetch it, boy, fetch it."

Petey Samson flopped down, and his hind paw itched behind his neck before he yawned at them.

"Maybe Isabel was right about he's a dud of a doggie," Alma said.

"He can't assist us this time, and we're on our own," Isabel said. "Where is it, Alma? Where should we search first?"

"Sorry, but I've got nothing to suggest," Alma replied.

"I'm feeling creeped out," Sammi Jo said. "Will the alarmed neighbors wonder about us spending so much time trespassing? Will they report us to Sheriff Fox who told us to stop our snooping?"

"Don't you just want to tell off the town busybodies?" Alma replied.

"I know exactly what you mean," Isabel said. "You can't do anything now without somebody gawking at you."

"Let's scoot before Sheriff Fox screeches up and yells at us," Sammi Jo said.

"We'll be returning here to track down Laura's diary," Isabel said. "You can hang your hat on it."

"Don't forget to put the windows back down and lock them," Alma said.

✎ ✎ ✎

Isabel, Alma, and Sammi Jo sat in Sheriff Fox's office while he appraised them from behind his shiny executive desk. A gold toothpick protruded from his grin. He leaned back in the chair, clasped his hands behind his head, and beamed his smug leer, infuriating Isabel.

"You rang us," Isabel said. "We came straight over as you requested. What's your earthshaking news?"

"Oh, it's nothing much except I located the murder weapon while I was poking around again in Farrah's Beauty Shop," Sheriff Fox replied. "I followed my cop's brilliant instincts, and there it was in her break room."

"What does Farrah have to say about it?" Isabel asked.

"I haven't confronted her with the evidence," Sheriff Fox replied.

"Show us the so-called evidence," Isabel said. "Where is it?"

"Not so fast, Isabel." Sheriff Fox was clearly enjoying himself by gloating at them. "I want to savor this special moment for a little while longer. Why you may ask? I finally beat Isabel and Alma at their sleuthing game. How sweet it is, too. I only wish I had a bottle of fizzy champagne to toast the big moment properly."

"You have ten seconds." Isabel's eyes blazed away. "Then we'll get up, walk out the door, and you'll never receive any help from any of us again."

"Give him both barrels loaded for bear, Isabel," Alma said.

Sheriff Fox stood up from the chair, reached for the bookshelf, and retrieved an object sealed inside a clear plastic evidence bag. The object resembled a slender tenpin used in a bowling alley. He dropped it on his desktop, making a solid clunk.

"Do you recognize what it is?" he asked.

"It's an Indian club," Isabel replied. "The wood is maple or possibly oak."

"Give the lady a cigar," Sheriff Fox said.

"I know what I'd like to give the gentleman," Alma muttered.

Sammi Jo smiled.

"The Indian club is fairly easy to grip, hoist up, and swing with lethal force." Sheriff Fox smirked. "So, I recovered the murder weapon, and you didn't find it. Well, well, aren't I the most clever one among us?"

"Where are Laura's bloodstains on it?" Isabel replied.

"Come again?" Sheriff Fox asked.

"The murder weapon used as a club should display lots of bloodstains," Isabel replied. "I observe none on it. Homicide is a messy affair."

"Obviously, Farrah wiped off the bloodstains," Sheriff Fox replied.

"H'm. When is the crime lab examining it?" Isabel asked.

"I'll look into it as soon as we adjourn," Sheriff Fox replied.

"We heard Farrah used Indian clubs in her home exercise program," Isabel said. "Why did she take this one to work with her?"

"Maybe she planned to exercise with it during her slow times," Sheriff Fox replied.

Isabel frowned. "I've never heard of a lady working out in a beauty shop. For starters, there isn't enough room to spread out and flail around without toppling over a chair or cracking a mirror."

"Farrah found a way," Sheriff Fox said. "If I had the time, I'd take you over to the beauty shop and demonstrate how you can exercise with the Indian club without any mishaps."

Alma looked sideways at Sammi Jo, and they burst out chortling before their hands covered up their mouths.

"Did I utter something funny?" Sheriff Fox asked.

"Hilarious even," Alma replied. "I'd pay an admission fee to watch you exercise with an Indian club."

"We town sheriffs don't have a sense of humor when it comes to dealing with a murder," Sheriff Fox said.

"We don't like town sheriffs who gloat over doing what's their job anyway," Isabel said.

"Maybe I was a little exuberant giving my update," Sheriff Fox said.

"Your big discovery doesn't excite or impress us," Isabel said.

"Why are you shooting down the best evidence I have to build my case and close out Laura's murder?" Sheriff Fox asked.

"Your so-called evidence is too obvious and convenient," Isabel replied. "If Farrah was the killer, she would've concealed the murder weapon in a better location or simply disposed of it. Just hang on to the Indian club, and we'll get back to you."

"I pin on the sheriff's badge, and I have the final say on everything," Sheriff Fox said. "My final say is Farrah Patel utilized this Indian club as the murder weapon to bludgeon Laura Isherwood over the head."

Isabel shook her head. "No, I don't think so."

"I agree with Isabel," Alma said.

"Mark me down the same way," Sammi Jo said.

"You're jealous because I found it, and you didn't look hard enough for it," Sheriff Fox said.

Isabel rolled her eyes a split second before Sammi Jo and Alma did.

"How about you congratulate me instead of rolling your eyes at me?" Sheriff Fox said.

"We've gone down this tortuous road before with you, Roscoe," Isabel said. "Remember how badly it turned out?"

"You end up having to backtrack and clean up the chaotic mess you created," Alma said.

"We have to help you clean it up," Isabel said. "We don't wish to go through it again."

"Are you pressing ahead?" Sheriff Fox asked.

"Hardly anybody will know we're sleuthing. We'll be as discreet as we possibly can be," Isabel replied.

"I'm prepared to leave here and arrest Farrah," Sheriff Fox said.

"We predict you'll come to regret it in short order," Isabel said.

"Then who in the blankety-blank is Laura's killer?" Sheriff Fox asked.

"I don't have the answer right here at my fingertips to give you," Isabel replied.

Sheriff Fox locked his eyes on Alma. "How soon can you get me the right answer?" he asked.

"I only wish I could give you a realistic timeframe," Alma replied.

"Why don't you give us a little more time?" Isabel said.

"How long do you need?" Sheriff Fox asked.

"Make it twenty-four hours," Isabel replied.

"You've got twelve hours," Sheriff Fox said.

"We'll get in touch with you after we know something," Isabel said.

"Be sure to leave your smartphone turned on," Alma said.

"Good idea," Sheriff Fox said as he did it.

Isabel, Alma, and Sammi Jo, heavily sighing together, left his office.

Chapter 15

"This is Bernie Wright. I received a strange email from Sammi Jane Garner, and she gave me this phone number. So, here I am calling it as she asked me to do."

Isabel's heartbeat took flight as the thrill of the chase galvanized her. Each time a new lead turned up, she resolved to press on and cross the finish line.

"She's Sammi Jo, not Sammi Jane, and I'm Isabel Trumbo. You may call me Isabel."

"It's swell to make your acquaintance, Isabel. Now would you mind telling me what this email is all about?"

Isabel told Bernie about the murder case in Quiet Anchorage, and how they were part of its investigation.

"Did you know your ex-sister-in-law Laura Isherwood?" Isabel asked.

"I heard Jodie mention Laura's name every once in a while, but I never met her," Bernie replied. "She didn't attend our wedding and never visited us in Richmond. She and Jodie didn't ever talk or text as far as I know. Jodie didn't hang up a framed photograph of Laura along with the rest of her family members on the wall."

"Jodie moved back to Quiet Anchorage after your divorce, and I've spoken to her over the last couple of days."

Bernie laughed. "Aren't you the lucky one then?"

"Really? She strikes me as a bright, poised young lady. My first impression of her was a favorable one."

"Yeah, she's a real sweetie pie until you try and live with her. Then she's a real piece of work, believe you me."

"I'm almost seventy-six-years old, and very little surprises me anymore."

"Jeez, you're old enough to be my grandmother, Isabel."

Isabel felt a jab of irritation. "Be that as it may, I'm interested in hearing your version of what happened in your failed marriage."

"Why should I share my sordid story with you?"

"Its details might prove useful, so I appeal to your sense of decency and fairness to help us bring Laura's murderer to justice."

"Tell me something. Is Jodie under suspicion?"

"As a close family member, she's considered a murder suspect."

"Then I'd put all my chips on she's the one who did it, and she deserves what she's got coming to her."

"Your thirst for revenge against your ex isn't very attractive. Can you give me the reason why you split up with her?"

"Money. That's it, pure and simple."

Isabel glanced at Alma who was closely following their conversation on the speakerphone.

"Money issues are one of the root causes for divorce," Isabel said. "Could I trouble you to elaborate a bit more?"

"Jodie spends money like it's going out of style," Bernie replied. "She racked up credit card debts, maxing them out. She emptied our joint savings account. I didn't see any end in sight, and I couldn't take her irresponsible behavior anymore, so I filed for divorce. Our day in court was a bloodletting, but I'll tell you this: I'm a happier man who sleeps a lot more restfully at night."

"Did she spend so impulsively before you were married? Didn't you know what trouble you were getting into?"

"She always had extravagant tastes, but we never had any real money back in the early days, so I didn't feel the pain until later."

"She appears to be improving. Could it be she's reformed and reined in her spending excesses? Folks do change, pardon the pun."

Bernie's scornful laugh was so harsh in Isabel's ear she grimaced.

"Don't let her fool you. Take my word for it. If Jodie gets a few dollars in her pocket, she isn't happy until it's spent and gone."

"What does she like to buy?"

"You name it. She's into new clothes and new shoes, loads of them."

Isabel smiled. "She doesn't sound a lot different than most of the young women I know."

Bernie repeated the laugh. "I've said my last word on my ex, so you can choose whether or not to believe me. Either way, it's no skin off my nose. Have we covered everything?"

"One last question and I'll let you go. Would Jodie murder Laura?"

"Truthfully, I don't know if Jodie would or not. She's a headstrong, manipulative woman, but I never saw her turn violent. We never came to physical blows during our quarrels, and the cops never hauled one of us away in handcuffs for domestic assault. But who knows? If she felt pressured or desperate enough, she might kill somebody. At this point, I sure wouldn't put it past her. That's about all I can tell you."

"Thank you for sharing your frank comments. They'll be helpful, I'm certain."

"Don't mention it," Bernie said.

"Enjoy the rest of your day," Isabel said before hanging up.

Isabel remembered she needed to make her phone call.

"Hello, Ossie. This is Isabel," she said on her smartphone. "How are you doing?"

"I'd know your lovely voice anywhere, Isabel," Ossie replied. "How nice of you to call me. Do you happen to like Belgian chocolates and red roses?"

"What lady doesn't like them? Why do you ask me?"

"Oh, it's nothing. Just call me a curious sort of a chap. What's going on?"

"Are you guys doing anything important?"

"We're sitting here swapping lies and swatting flies."

"I'm looking for a few warm bodies to play Scrabble with me. My attempt to teach Petey Samson went nowhere."

"Has Alma left town? We haven't gotten word of it."

"She doddered on back to her bedroom to lie down and take her nap with Petey Samson."

"I'd love to come over and play Scrabble with you. But, you see, well,..."

"Well, what is it exactly, Ossie?"

"Willie should be the one to speak to you. He's better at explaining this stuff than I am."

"Put him on the phone then."

"Hi, Isabel. I just overheard you speaking to Ossie."

"I'm rounding up a few Scrabble partners, Willie. Are you available?"

"Here's the deal. We're taking our catnaps this afternoon to stock up on our sleep. Tonight we rendezvous in the piney woods armed with our telescopes, infrared cameras, and ice chest filled with Nehi sodas."

Isabel felt a flash of annoyance. "Don't tell me you're trekking out there to go UFO spotting."

"After a hiatus, the UFOs are supposed to be flying in force tonight, which is sweet music to my ears."

"Aren't you afraid the little green men may swoop down and abduct you?"

"Our tinfoil hats, welding goggles, and hazmat suits will protect us."

Isabel laughed at the comical image. "Do they work?"

"All I can tell you is I haven't been abducted once while I wore mine."

"There is always the first time for everything, Willie."

Willie snickered under his breath. "I always stand *behind* Blue and Ossie any time I'm in the piney woods."

"You guys can go UFO spotting tomorrow night."

"Sorry, but tomorrow night is a risky time. The meteorologist predicts a fifty percent chance of thunderstorms which keeps the UFOs grounded in the cargo bays of the mother ship."

"That truly stinks if I may say so."

"All is not lost. Perhaps we can make it work out. What if we drop by tomorrow night and play Scrabble with you?"

"I could sit still for that. Nothing is more atmospheric than a noisy, flashy thunderstorm during a Scrabble match. If the electric power goes out, we'll light a few candles and keep on playing until dawn in a marathon session. Willie, you're an absolute gem!"

"Thank you for noticing, Isabel. I've been telling Ossie and Blue the same thing for years, and I've gotten nowhere with them."

"I'm sure they'll come around. Be sure you bring them with you tomorrow night at seven o'clock sharp. I'll have on hand all the iced tea you can drink."

"Splendid. Will you also be serving bear claws?"

"They're Alma's department, but I'll mention it to her. She'll probably have a platter of them to offer you."

"Then it's a date. Oh yeah, there's one last item before I forget it."

"You'd better tell me then."

"Make certain the Q, X, and Z letter tiles aren't missing, and Alma isn't stashing them up her sleeve or under her watchband."

"Don't you worry about Alma for one second," Isabel said. "I've been wise to her shady shenanigans since we grew up on the farm, and I'll keep a sharp eye on her."

"We'll be there with bells on our toes. See you tomorrow night," Willie said.

"I'm already tingling from the excitement," Isabel said.

"We have to wind up Laura's murder mystery before tomorrow night," Isabel later told Alma while they sat at the dining room table. "I can't play Scrabble with it preying on my mind and disrupting my concentration while I'm spelling out my words on the game board."

"You should've discussed it with me before you set it up," Alma said. "We're no closer to winding it up now than we were yesterday at this time."

Isabel quirked her lips. "I'd rather gag on a spoon than cancel our Scrabble game. We have to pick up the pace and make better progress."

"Repeat what Bernie told you on the phone."

"He swore Jodie spent every dime they ever earned and rang up extravagant credit card debts. She was unable to learn the concept of thriftiness, and he couldn't bear it any longer, so they divorced and went their separate ways."

"Is she any better now with taking care of her personal finances?"

"From all outward appearances, she's gotten a handle on them."

"How can we ask Jodie our follow-up questions? Trapping her on her way into the bank again probably won't be as successful."

Isabel nodded. "Even so, it's still our best chance to grab her attention."

Alma held up Tallulah's door key. "But first we made plans to revisit Laura's rented townhouse. Now is as good a time as any to go back and try our luck."

"Petey Samson can stay home and take his nap," Isabel said. "He's more taken with munching on the tortilla chips than he is with sniffing out the clues. If Sammi Jo isn't tied up, maybe she can go with us."

The evening was late enough to lure out the fireflies but still too light to hear the whippoorwills' eponymous yelps sound from the piney woods and honeysuckle tangles. Sammi Jo had arrived before Isabel and Alma pulled up. Sammi Jo arose from sitting on the porch step as Isabel and Alma strolled over from the parked car.

"Did you bring your magnifying glasses?" Sammi Jo asked.

"Each of us came equipped with one," Alma replied. "Isabel saw to it."

"One of us has to be the responsible one," Isabel said.

"Did you also remember to put a Maglite in your pocketbook, Oh Great Responsible One?" Alma asked. "Or will you use your owl eyes to guide us through the dark rooms in the townhouse?"

"A Maglite won't be necessary," Isabel replied. "We'll switch on the electric lights. I've had it prowling around as if we're cat burglars. Tallulah gave us her permission to be here, and we don't care what the neighbors or Sheriff Fox thinks."

Once inside the townhouse, they headed into Laura's bedroom.

"Where did Laura stash her diary?" Isabel asked, glancing at Sammi Jo. "Any ideas?"

"Don't ask me," Sammi Jo replied. "I don't have the patience and aptitude to sit down every night and write a diary entry."

"I'm with Sammi Jo," Alma said. "Keeping a diary is monotonous as doing homework."

"Right and watching soap operas provides such edge-of-your-seat excitement," Isabel said.

"Stop picking on my soap operas," Alma said.

"Don't you ever grow tired of watching them?" Isabel asked.

"Do you ever grow tired of eating or breathing?" Alma replied.

"What a nincompoop response," Isabel said.

"The last thing we need to deal with right now is a sister's tiff over soap operas," Sammi Jo said. "We came to hunt for Laura's diary, and that's all."

"Do you have a screwdriver to remove the wall vent cover?" Isabel asked.

"You never can tell because I just might," Alma replied as she brandished her hefty pocketbook. "If I do have a screwdriver, it's probably settled to the bottom. Shall I look for it?"

"Yes, please do," Isabel replied.

Heaving out a weary groan, Alma plopped down on the army cot. She undid the brass clasp, turned her pocketbook upside-down, and shook it. Lip balm, safety pins, and a rabbit's foot rained down. She jiggled it harder as a magnifying glass, portable smartphone charger, and hand sanitizer container spilled out. Isabel swiped her smartphone screens while she waited.

Alma wasn't finished. Seven Rice Krispies bars, six apples, and five packets of caramelized sunflower seeds followed, tumbling down and making the pile larger. Isabel patted back a yawn as Alma continued emptying her pocketbook. Restraining from making a snarky comment, Isabel tapped her toe. Alma dumped out the rest of the items--why did she carry a crow caller?--from it. Finally, the last item, a butter knife, landed on the army cot.

"Whew, I need to take a break," Alma said, wiping off her brow.

"After making it into a big production, do you see a screwdriver?" Isabel asked.

"Hold your horses, and I'll see if I do." Alma poked her finger through the various items in the pile, starting with the butter knife. "I regret to inform you I brought no screwdriver."

Isabel groaned. "Alma, you could try the patience of a snail."

"We've determined I didn't bring a screwdriver," Alma said. "We'll move on to implementing Plan B."

"Why on earth would I have a Plan B ready?" Isabel asked.

"Plan B is looking again in the kitchen," Sammi Jo said.

"We'll help Alma cram her stuff back into her pocketbook," Isabel said.

"Would you also like a Rice Krispies bar or apple?" Alma asked.

"I'm not hungry, thanks," Isabel said.

"Sammi Jo?" Alma asked.

"Thanks, but I had a Slim Jim, pork rinds, and RC Cola before I came over," Sammi Jo replied.

"That's all right," Alma said. "It leaves more for me."

They trooped downstairs, Isabel flipped on the electric lights, and they entered the kitchen.

"Did you look in the refrigerator's top freezer?" Alma asked.

Isabel did so but with no luck. "Guess again where Laura's hiding place is."

"I don't see a toaster or breadbox," Alma said.

"Is any section of the toe kick panel detachable?" Isabel asked.

Sammi Jo got down on fours and grappled with the toe kick panel under the kitchen cabinets. She was unable to pop out any short section and expose a secret cavity Laura had created. While rising to her feet, Sammi Jo had an idea.

"The crisper drawer might be worth a look," Sammi Jo said.

Isabel pulled open the fridge door, tugged out the crisper drawer, and her face brightened with a smile. "Bingo!" She held up a pink diary secured by a strap and silver-toned lock. It was small enough to fit inside a pocketbook or a fanny pack.

"Hurray! Sammi Jo gets our hearty kudos and thanks," Alma said.

"Well shucks, I just took a wild guess," Sammi Jo said. "How do we unlock it?"

"I don't see the key," Isabel said while inspecting the crisper drawer and refrigerator shelves.

"We don't have the time to comb through the townhouse looking for the small key," Alma said.

"Then we'll figure out how to get into it after we leave here," Isabel said.

Chapter 16

Gathered around the dining room table were Isabel, Alma, Sammi Jo, and Petey Samson, who was more of a panhandler for doggie treats than he was a sleuth. However, his major benefactor, Isabel, had focused her energies on a different matter. Arrayed in front of her on the table were the various tools--a bobby pin, a bent paperclip, and a paring knife with the tip broken off after she tried using it to spring open the lock on Laura Isherwood's pink diary. All the while, Alma fidgeted in the chair.

"Let me take another crack at it," Alma said. "I think I figured out how to get it open."

"You already took your turn, Alma," Isabel said. "Now we have to buy a new paring knife thanks to you."

"Then it's Sammi Jo's turn, and she'll let me take it," Alma said.

"How difficult can it be to pick the chintzy lock on a diary?" Isabel asked.

"Just tear or cut off the plastic strap," Sammi Jo replied.

"We don't want anybody to know we read it," Isabel said. "It's too grubby even by our standards."

"Laura won't mind if we read it with the purpose in mind to bring her killer to justice," Alma said.

"Alma makes a lot of sense," Sammi Jo said.

"I've reached my frustration threshold," Isabel said. "Here you go. You can take it." She forwarded the diary to Sammi Jo. "Use brute force and open it."

Sammi Jo yanked off the plastic strap with the lock and handed the diary back to Isabel. She flipped over its front cover, licked her thumb, and leafed through its crinkly pages. After stopping at the first handwritten page, she squinted and bit her bottom lip. Then she moved the diary further away from her eyes and squinted harder. Next, she drew up the diary to within a few inches from the tip of her nose and swerved her eyes precariously close together.

"Shall I go fetch your reading glasses?" Alma asked.

"Sammi Jo with her 20/20 vision can read it aloud," Isabel replied while she returned the diary.

Sammi Jo trained her young eyes on the page and deciphered the spidery cursive handwriting. "Laura used a slew of exclamation points and smiley faces. I did the same thing when I was in junior high school, but then I outgrew it."

"Laura never wore a smiley face button when I saw her at the beauty shop," Alma said.

"Skim through her diary entries and give us what she wrote about her marriage," Isabel said. "Any places where she refers to Deacon are of particular interest."

"Her diary begins on May fifteenth, and she records something in it daily," Sammi Jo said as she browsed through the handwritten pages.

"Does she open each record with the ever-popular 'Dear Diary' salutation?" Alma asked.

"Believe it or not, she does. She ends each record with 'Till the next time.'" Sammi Jo laughed. "Isn't that goofy as all get out?"

Isabel smiled. "What compelled Laura to leave Deacon and go live on her own?"

"Give me a few more minutes," Sammi Jo replied. "I'm not the fast reader like you and Alma are with reading your mysteries. Laura reports she gets nightly migraine headaches, but she's stubborn about not taking off any sick days from the beauty shop. She needs to keep her job and stay on good terms with her boss Farah."

"We know they had their differences," Isabel said. "Laura was often in Farrah's doghouse."

"Their conflicts didn't rise to the level of committing murder," Alma said.

"Farrah said they quarreled in private, and nobody saw them," Isabel said.

"She was Laura's boss, and bosses sometimes get angry with their employees," Alma said.

"Yes, Alma, I remember how bosses can be from my days as a professional lady," Isabel said. "My memory hasn't started to slip."

"Skip over the rest and read her diary entry about Deacon's company picnic," Alma said.

"I just found it," Sammi Jo said.

"Did they argue over her attending the company picnic with him?" Isabel asked.

"She's rather cryptic in her entry," Sammi Jo replied. "She writes Deacon has been sleeping on the sofa, and they haven't spoken to each other in several weeks."

"Does she give the reason for their estrangement?" Isabel asked.

"Again, she doesn't come right out with providing the nitty-gritty details," Sammi Jo replied.

"You'd think she would record them in her diary," Alma said.

"What are you, our resident expert on diaries?" Isabel asked. "You've never even kept one."

"I expect I know every bit as much about keeping a diary as you do," Alma replied.

"You can't even write down the doggie treats we need on the grocery-shopping list," Isabel said.

"Endowed with a prodigious memory, I can remember them," Alma said.

"Pardon the interruption, Sammi Jo," Isabel said. "Continue, please."

"Laura reveals her suspicions that Deacon is having an affair, but she doesn't write down who the other woman is," Sammi Jo said.

"She had a justification for shooting the two-timing polecat," Alma said.

"Alma, let's not lose sight of our cool objectivity," Isabel said.

"Just saying," Alma said. "Anyway, we don't need to delve any deeper to find the wedge that drove apart their marriage."

"She only speculates Deacon is running around on her," Isabel said. "However, she offers no proof of it."

"She was no dummy. She knew where there's smoke there's fire," Alma said. "I've been burned the same way as she was, and it's no fun."

"Where does she first mention the townhouse she rented from Tallulah?" Isabel asked.

"Right after the company picnic, Laura writes Tallulah stopped by the beauty shop," Sammi Jo replied. "They settled on the monthly rent, and Laura says she feels more hopeful than she has in a long time."

"Have her migraine headaches improved any now that she's made up her mind to strike out on her own?" Isabel asked.

Sammi Jo used her finger to trace under the handwritten words as she read them.

"She writes she's nothing but thrilled to get away from Deacon's nasty temper," Sammi Jo replied. "She raises her fears of what he'll do once he discovers her intentions to leave him."

"Does she write he could use violence to oppose her?" Isabel asked.

Sammi Jo nodded. "Laura writes and I quote, 'Deacon is getting impossible to live with anymore. He stalks around the house at all hours of the night, keeping me awake. By now, I'm deathly afraid of him. I think he might be hiding a handgun somewhere in the house.'"

"If Deacon had a handgun, why didn't he use it to kill her?" Isabel asked.

"Maybe he forgot where he put the handgun," Alma replied.

Isabel looked dubious.

"Or, if he did remember, maybe he didn't have any bullets to load it with," Alma said.

Isabel looked more dubious. "Give us the rest of it, Sammi Jo," she said.

"Laura writes she wonders who she can turn to and confide in about her marriage troubles," Sammi Jo said.

"Does she mull over whether or not to tell her older sister Jodie?" Isabel asked.

"Laura doesn't mention any possible confidantes she feels she can trust with her story," Sammi Jo replied.

"She could have come to see Isabel and me," Alma said. "We're known in Quiet Anchorage for assisting the folks who are distressed."

"We've discussed how she was too private a person to approach anybody with her difficulties," Isabel said.

"It's better late than never, so we're in her corner now," Alma said.

"There you go then," Isabel said. "So we are."

"Her diary entries abruptly end the day before her murder," Sammi Jo said, closing the diary.

"Why didn't she write the diary entry on her last night alive?" Alma asked. "She faithfully adhered to her daily schedule up until then."

Isabel shrugged. "Maybe she had a terrible migraine headache, took something for it, and went to bed early. What do you think, Sammi Jo?"

"I don't know, but the plot sure has thickened with our reading Laura's diary," Sammi Jo replied.

"You know it, too," Isabel said. "Her diary has to count as our first substantial clue."

"My idea to look in the crisper drawer paid big dividends," Alma said.

"It was Sammi Jo's idea," Isabel said.

"Oh, so it was," Alma said. "Well, I seconded her idea."

They traveled over the dark country road again, the car windows open. Isabel enjoyed listening to the high-pitched drone of the night insects. She closed her eyes and let herself drift away, but not too far away because the murder case always loomed there in front of her. Going around or over it was impossible. Then a jolt of excitement told her the end had come within sight. However, they mustn't let down their guard. She reiterated her warning.

"We have to exercise more caution at night," she said. "Thankfully, Alma and I can see sharper after our cataract surgery."

"It's the healthiest thing I've done for myself since I included more fiber in my diet," Alma said.

"We can leave your high-fiber diet topic right there," Isabel replied. "What did Blaine tell you when you saw him earlier, Sammi Jo?"

"After thinking more about it, he swears Deacon didn't murder Laura," Sammi Jo replied.

"Blaine is Deacon's old friend and will stick up for him," Alma said. "Did you bring Laura's diary?"

"I put it in my pocketbook," Isabel replied as she patted it.

"We'll ask Deacon a few pointed questions," Sammi Jo said.

"Did you bring your pocketbook derringer in the event things turn unruly?" Isabel asked.

"I never leave home without it," Sammi Jo replied.

"Do you know how to let off the safety thingamajig?" Isabel asked.

"Just know I'm skilled in its use," Sammi Jo replied.

"Is it loaded with more than the one bullet?" Isabel asked. "We'll probably need at least three or perhaps four bullets. What do you think, Alma?"

"Sammi Jo says she has everything under control," Alma replied. "Will you quit fretting as a mother hen does over her chicks?"

"We didn't call Sheriff Fox about recovering Laura's diary," Isabel said. "Why didn't we notify him, Alma? You were supposed to remind me of it."

"Because he's snoring away while he's stretched out in his recliner with the TV blaring," Alma replied. "If we have to wake him up, let's make sure it's for a good reason since he'll probably go ballistic."

"Roscoe should go ballistic every so often," Isabel said. "It gets the blood pumping through his veins and sharpens his police smarts."

"He also provides us with lowbrow entertainment but don't tell him I said so," Alma said.

The interior lights brightened the front windows at the Isherwoods' cottage. Deacon had also turned on the porch lights flanking the front door. They parked in the driveway and cobbled together a plan.

"Hopefully, Deacon won't mind us knocking on his door this late," Isabel said.

"Wasn't he asking about us in town?" Alma asked. "Blue phoned us and said as much."

"Then we have the perfect excuse to be here tonight," Isabel said.

"If you want, I'll do the door knocking," Sammi Jo said.

"What on earth would we do without Sammi Jo?" Isabel said.

"It's a team effort," Sammi Jo said. "I'm doing my part."

Sammi Jo took care of the door-knocking duties.

"You're wasting your time." The tall, gaunt Deacon dressed in black like a pallbearer gave them his menacing glower. He'd shaved and paid for a haircut. Nonetheless, he still looked as if he'd been dragged backward through a knothole. "As I told you when you came with Blaine, I did *not* kill Laura, and that's my final word on it. You may as well hightail it on back to town and leave me alone."

"A couple of new developments have arisen since we last talked," Isabel said.

"I suppose you want to bring me up to speed," Deacon said.

"You'll find them as compelling as we do," Isabel said.

"What I heard was Sheriff Fox is arresting Laura's boss Farrah," Deacon said. "Didn't you hear the same buzz? It's the latest talk of the town."

"He'll make a bogus arrest if he goes through with it," Isabel replied. "Farrah is innocent, and she didn't kill your wife. We're virtually certain of it."

Deacon frowned a little. "You can begin by elaborating more."

"Sheriff Fox's arrest of Farrah won't hold up," Sammi Jo said. "We've been through this drill with him on the previous murder cases."

"Are you Ray Burl's daughter?" Deacon asked. "You look just like him. Ray Burl was a friend of mine."

"Ray Burl was my dad." Sammi Jo spoke in a softer voice. "His murder is one of the reasons why I do this sleuthing stuff. The mosquitoes are eating us up. Shall we go indoors and sit down in the comfort of your living room?"

"Are you sure about doing that?" Deacon said. "I might break bad and bump you off. I am a cold-blooded killer, after all."

Sammi Jo laughed.

"Come on in, you all," Deacon said, stepping aside and ushering them through the doorway. "I'll listen to what you have to say."

"Good deal," Sammi Jo replied.

The ladies claimed the couch while Deacon sank into his recliner. He aimed the TV remote and turned off the TV program. No playing cards or soda cans were visible.

"Let me in on your new developments," he said.

"Did you know Laura kept a diary she'd written in every day since the middle of May?" Isabel asked.

"You're way off base," Deacon replied. "She didn't write down anything, not even a laundry list."

"Nonetheless, she did record her thoughts and feelings," Isabel said. "She writes very intriguing things about you."

"Give me the most intriguing thing you got," Deacon said.

"She accuses you of carrying on an affair," Isabel said.

"That's an outright lie." Deacon's eyes bulged, and his lean face hardened. "I never messed around on Laura. I have my share of warts, sure, but I remained faithful despite the growing rift in our marriage. Who did I have my alleged tryst with?"

"She doesn't spell out the name," Isabel replied.

"Of course she hasn't since there wasn't nobody," Deacon said.

"Perhaps she hadn't gotten that far in sussing it out," Isabel said. "Given enough time, she would've named the other woman."

"I never saw the other woman," Deacon said. "Do you have her diary? Where did she write down all this garbage?"

Isabel removed Laura's diary from her pocketbook. "Does it look familiar?" Isabel held it up like a flashcard and turned it for him to see the front and rear covers.

"I've never laid eyes on it until now," Deacon replied. "The diaries are sold at the five-and-dime where I've seen teenage girls buy them. Laura never had a diary. Why did you break into it?"

"Reading what she wrote was important to pursuing her murder investigation," Isabel replied. "Why did she plan to leave you?"

"She was upset with me over a few personal issues," Deacon replied.

"Are you prepared to tell us what the personal issues were?" Isabel asked.

"Can you give me a legitimate reason why you need to know?" Deacon replied.

"We've ventured this far with our discussion," Isabel said. "Why stop now?"

"With a hair-trigger temper, I've been known to fly into rages, which I come to regret later," Deacon said. "I end up making apologies and promising to do better the next time."

"You're in fair control of your ungovernable temper now despite my pelting you with our questions," Isabel said.

"I'm emotionally drained from the past few grueling days, and I have no energy left to quarrel with you," Deacon said.

"What else besides your temper made your marriage run off the rails?" Isabel asked.

"Laura and I weren't communicating," Deacon replied. "Before long, I was sleeping out here on the sofa. She claimed I wasn't showing her my genuine emotions. You know, I wasn't sensitive and reflective enough to meet her needs." He shrugged. "I can't rewire my personality. Or maybe I didn't try hard enough."

"Laura reveals her fear you hid a handgun in the house," Isabel said.

"I detest handguns, and I wouldn't own one," Deacon said.

"She emphasizes she's afraid of how you'd react if you discovered her plan to pack up and leave," Isabel said.

"Again, it's pure fiction," Deacon said. "Laura told me she was moving out into the townhouse she'd rented from Tallulah Pettigrew."

"Were you agreeable to the separation?" Isabel asked.

"Getting the news didn't thrill me, but my trying to block her would've done no good," Deacon replied. "She'd made up her mind. Look, I still loved her, and I kept my hopes alive we'd patch up things and salvage our marriage. We'd talked about starting a family. I considered getting us into couples therapy or taking a long vacation. But then I ran out of time."

"Why are there inconsistencies between what you're telling us, and what her diary says?" Isabel asked.

"How should I know?" Deacon replied. "Let me take a look at it." Isabel hesitated.

"Lend it to him, Isabel," Alma said. "I trust him to treat it with care."

"I'll read what she wrote and return it to you," Deacon said.

Isabel handed Laura's diary to Deacon who flipped it open and scanned its contents. He leaned in closer to the brightness from the table lamp. A few minutes crawled by as he read on, deliberately and slowly absorbing it.

He flipped to the next page and frowned. As the next minutes dragged by, he turned the pages, read further entries, and scowled. He grunted. Isabel and Alma exchanged baffled glances. He stopped reading, his sallow face left grim. His voice coarsened.

"This diary you brought me with your questions is one hundred percent fake." Deacon slapped it shut. "You've been duped."

"Come again?" Isabel said.

"Laura isn't the author of this alleged diary." Deacon gave Isabel an earnest look. "It's a forgery, a counterfeit diary. There's no question about it."

"How do you figure?" Isabel asked.

"The handwriting style matches Laura's from what I can tell," Deacon replied. "But the date is wrong. Our company picnic was on June *fourth*, not on June fifth. She wouldn't slip up on the detail, especially after we bickered over her not going to it."

"Mr. Dunfee also gave us the June fourth date for the company picnic," Isabel said. "Anything else?"

"As I already stated, my owning the handgun is a falsehood," Deacon replied. "Laura never drew these cutesy smiley faces. Then the fake Laura claims she suffers from bad migraine headaches every night. My Laura came down with them once, maybe twice a month, but it was never a nightly event, thank goodness. Do you follow me?"

"We'll let you know if we don't," Isabel said.

"A few other details are total fabrications," Deacon said. "Laura was never frightened of me, as it states here, and I never threatened her. I practically fell on my knees and begged her to stay. As I just said, my extra-marital fling never took place."

"Was Laura writing down things she thought were true but weren't grounded in reality?" Isabel asked. "Was she delusional?"

"She was perfectly rational when I spoke to her," Deacon replied. "Something else. The diary entries appear daily except on the last night of her life. She was meticulous in everything she did, and she wouldn't have skipped writing for the one night."

"I had the same reaction to the missing final entry," Alma said.

"You present a persuasive argument." Isabel sought Alma's concurrence.

Alma smiled. "You're probably spot-on. We recovered the evidence the forger intentionally planted in the crisper drawer. He or she put the fake diary there for the police to recover only we did."

"The frame job is rickety as old scaffolding but serves its purpose," Isabel said.

"Somebody in Quiet Anchorage set me up to take the fall for Laura's murder." Raking his fingers through his hair, Deacon's voice cracked. "If I've made enemies hating me that much, it's news to me."

"Somebody expended a lot of effort," Isabel said. "Who created the phony diary?"

"Examine it from this angle," Alma replied. "Whose handwriting most closely resembles Laura's?"

"Jodie Wright," Isabel replied. "The handwriting styles of two sisters can look alike. Only we can tell the subtle differences in ours."

"You just stated why Jodie gets my vote," Alma said.

"So, Jodie killed her younger sister and my wife in cold blood." Deacon shook his head in bewilderment. "Ain't that a kick in the head?" He set his vivid blue eyes on Isabel. "You're the detectives. Why did Jodie commit murder? What did she have against either of us?"

"We don't know the reason yet," Isabel replied. "Give us a little more time, and we can dig it up."

"You seem to have more on the ball than Sheriff Fox does," Deacon said.

"There ain't no seems about it," Sammi Jo said. "Isabel and Alma find the right answers on every murder case."

Deacon nodded. "Good, good. I like hearing it."

"Here's the thing, Deacon," Isabel fixed her steady gaze on him. "You can't get involved. Stay away from Jodie and don't take matters into your own hands. You can't win that way. You only lose by going to prison, and you don't want to spend the rest of your life behind bars. Do we have an agreement?"

"Yeah, okay, I can wait," Deacon replied as he handed the diary back to Isabel. "Just make it quick because my patience is burning on a short fuse."

"Take care now," Isabel said.

As they were stepping out the front door, Deacon burst out weeping, his guttural wails and sobs agonizing. Sammi Jo darted a glance over her shoulder. He'd covered his face with his hands. His chest convulsed before he heaved for air.

"We can't leave him in that shape," Sammi Jo said.

"We don't have time to pick up the pieces for him," Alma said.

"Blaine should be at the hardware store," Isabel said, her smartphone in hand. "They're friends."

"Our role is to find his wife's murderer for Sheriff Fox to arrest," Alma said.

Isabel gave an affirmative nod. "We're getting closer. I can feel it."

Chapter 17

For the first time in recent memory, Sammi Jo drove the car with Isabel riding in the passenger seat, and Alma sitting behind Isabel. She told Sammi Jo they couldn't multitask by driving a car while on the final phase of a murder case. They left Deacon's house on the windy, dark road leading into Quiet Anchorage.

"Follow the money trail," Isabel said. "Isn't it one of the detective's golden rules?"

"So what if it is?" Alma said.

"When Bernie Wright phoned me, he said his ex spent most of their money," Isabel said. "Jodie never changed her destructive habit, so he ended their marriage. My theory is she's in similar financial straits, and yet she drives a nice car, and she wears nice clothes. She told us she recently went clothes shopping at the mall with Laura."

"How does the perpetually broke Jodie manage to pay for her nice things?" Alma asked.

"You pose the right question," Isabel said. "Now let's deliberate on it. What's your most logical answer?"

"She has another source of income," Alma replied.

"What is her other source of income?" Isabel asked. "Where does she get her extra cash?"

"Did she win a big jackpot in the Virginia lottery?" Alma replied.

"You make a credible guess, but in Jodie's case focus on something shady and crooked," Isabel said.

"Has she been embezzling money from her employer Archie Blevins at the lumberyard?" Alma replied. "Is that where you're going with your theory?"

"It merits our serious consideration," Isabel replied.

Alma nodded. "If Archie isn't monitoring his finances, Jodie might be cooking the books while she's cleaning him out."

"She's devised a clandestine scheme to rob him and his business," Isabel said.

"He's grown to trust her enough to let her do the bookkeeping with no oversight or audits," Alma said.

"No boss should be so naive and neglectful," Isabel said.

"Notify Sheriff Fox we're going after Jodie," Alma said.

Isabel used her smartphone and reached Abigail Morgan Pierpont, Sheriff Fox's smart administrative assistant who provided the skills to keep his office running as efficiently as it did.

"Sheriff Fox is in a closed-door meeting," Abigail said.

"Is his meeting about Laura's murder case?" Isabel asked.

"It's about him consuming his coffee and doughnuts. He tasked me with screening his calls. I don't like doing it, but the pay is the same."

"You're due for a pay raise if he's having you cover for him while he's gorging on coffee and doughnuts."

Abigail laughed. "Hold the phone, and I'll put you through. If he barks at me, I'll just bark back louder."

"Tell him Isabel wants a word," Isabel said. "He'll take my call, no questions asked."

After a short wait, Sheriff Fox sounded like he was eating. "Isabel, every time you or Alma ring my office, I can feel my blood pressure going through the roof."

"It's more likely due to the caffeine buzz from all the cups of coffee you drink," Isabel said.

"I hope you're not pestering me with anything to do with the Laura Isherwood homicide since I'm set to officially close it."

"True to form, you act too hastily and arrest the wrong person. I stand behind what I said previously. Farrah Patel is innocent of Laura's murder."

"Did Alma put you up to this? Are you messing with me?"

"Roscoe, you know we're nothing but serious when it comes to murder."

"We've reached the part in our script where I'm supposed to ask you why you think Farrah isn't the murderer. Okay, why isn't she?"

"Because we think Jodie Wright is looking a lot guiltier for it." "Now I'm supposed to drop everything I'm doing and dash off to arrest Jodie Wright instead. Well, here's a newsflash. I'm going off-script, and I'm not doing it. The murder weapon is Farrah's Indian club, and I sent it off to the crime lab. When I receive their crime report, I'm placing Farrah under arrest. Heed my orders and back off. You got it plain wrong this time."

"Be the usual mule-headed town sheriff and see if I give a hoot in a high wind. I've told you the truth. We can't be responsible for what you choose to do with it."

"I'll leave on my smartphone for any further developments from you. That's the best I can do."

"Whoopee and thanks a million. If I get a free moment, I'll give you a holler, but I wouldn't hold my breath if I were you. Goodbye." Isabel spoke over her shoulder. "Why have we been cursed with a dolt for a town sheriff?"

"We helped to get him elected," Alma replied.

"Don't remind me of it," Isabel said. "I fulfilled our obligation to inform him of our activities."

"If he decides to ignore us, we can't change his mind," Alma said.

"Sammi Jo, I'd tell you to step on it for the lumberyard," Isabel said. "However, I know you tend to put the pedal to the metal anyway."

Sammi Jo chuckled. "I'll take it easy with my lead foot so as not to give my two passengers a heart attack."

"We sure do thank you for sparing our hearts," Isabel said.

The lumberyard when they pulled in was closed and buttoned up for the night. The parking area had no cars, and no interior lights illuminated any of the office windows. Isabel remembered Jodie had told them she put in a lot of work hours. Was she using the overtime to "cook the books," as Alma had put it, and swindled her boss?

Isabel had no idea where Jodie lived in town, so their next logical move was to sit, watch the lumberyard, and catch Jodie if she returned. Sammi Jo had maneuvered the car into a secluded nook between the stacked lumber affording them a wide view of the office building. They got settled and waited in the quiet darkness.

Soon the snoring was like that of a boar hog sleeping in a mud wallow. Jarred out of her reverie, Isabel wanted to insert her earplugs and close her bedroom door except she wasn't at home. The next snore almost rattled the car windows and windshield in their frames. She gave Sammi Jo a sideways look, but she was awake.

"Is that Alma snoring?" Sammi Jo asked.

"Who else do you think it is? Me?" Isabel replied.

"She has a wicked snore," Sammi Jo said.

"No wonder she dozes off at the drop of a hat," Isabel said. "She stays up half the night reading her mysteries and playing with Petey Samson."

"She's told me you do the same thing," Sammi Jo said.

Isabel sniffed. "However, when I fall asleep I make ladylike, dainty noises."

"Are you going to prod her awake?" Sammi Jo asked.

"You've never had to face Alma when she first wakes up," Isabel said. "I'd rather take my chances facing an enraged bull in the bullring."

"We'll grit our teeth and put up with her wicked snoring as well as we can," Sammi Jo said.

"Your wise suggestion is our best course of action," Isabel said.

After her vociferous yawn and stretching her arms, Alma piped up from the rear seat. "I must've drifted off and taken a catnap."

"Did you?" Isabel said with a straight face. "We hadn't noticed."

Repressing her snickers, Sammi Jo refused to look at Isabel and crack up laughing.

"Did I miss anything important?" Alma asked.

"Some detective you are falling asleep on the job," Isabel replied.

"Maybe you should take a catnap, too," Alma said. "It might improve your cranky disposition."

"I'm no crankier than I usually am," Isabel said.

Sammi Jo's ringing smartphone interrupted their fussing.

"Who can that be at this time of night?" she asked, checking. "Oh no, it's Reynolds."

"In all the uproar, I'd forgotten about him," Isabel said.

"Join the club," Sammi Jo said before she greeted him.

"What do you want, Reynolds? Tell me in as few words as possible. I'm a little busy here."

"You'll like hearing what I have to say. I've settled on our wedding date."

"A likely story is all I can say."

"Huh? I thought you'd be thrilled down to your toes to hear my news."

"You caught me at a bad time."

"I don't like the sound of that. What's up?"

"I'm with Isabel and Alma taking care of business. Put that in your pipe and smoke it."

"Uh-huh. You're busy playing detective again just as I suspected."

"Hey, you like to watch the fast cars zipping around in a large oval, and I like to play a lady detective. Different strokes, babe. We're all weird in our unique way."

"What should I do about our wedding date?"

"Hold the thought until we can discuss it later when I'm not so distracted."

"Your facing dangerous situations like now makes it hard for me not to worry."

"We only take calculated risks and watch our backs all the time," Sammi Jo said. "I have to go now. Duty calls. Take care, love."

Sammi Jo did a fist pump for Isabel and Alma.

"Reynolds wants to get married," Sammi Jo said. "All we have to do is firm up the wedding date."

"Even so, I should offer you a word of caution," Alma said. "Marriage isn't usually a done deal until after you return from your honeymoon and settle into your daily routines."

"Quit spreading your doom and gloom. Be happy for Sammi Jo," Isabel said. "You're only a first-time bride once in your life."

"As expected, I'm ecstatic over Sammi Jo's impending nuptials," Alma said. "I'm just saying don't throw caution to the wind."

"Shall I pin on the family heirloom you gave me to my wedding sash?" Sammi Jo asked.

"You'll look radiant and stunning if you do or don't pin it on," Isabel replied.

"We told you about its fertility charms," Alma said. "You'll be taking your chances later on your honeymoon if you decide to pin it to your wedding sash."

"Then I'll keep it in my jewelry box to wear after our honeymoon," Sammi Jo said.

"You'll have plenty of time," Isabel said.

"Something Roscoe told us earlier bugs me," Alma replied.

"I take everything he says with an extra grain of salt," Isabel said. "What's bugging you?"

"He swears up and down Farrah is the guilty culprit who murdered Laura," Alma replied.

"Just because he says it doesn't make it true," Isabel said.

"What if he's right this time?" Alma asked. "Suppose Farrah is Laura's killer. Suppose we're plunging down the wrong rabbit hole. Suppose we're off-target."

"He asked us to give him a hand," Isabel replied. "That's all we're doing out here tonight."

"I know it's unlikely, but we may have blown it," Alma said. "You have to admit we're not infallible."

"We've come this far, Alma, so we can hardly stop now," Isabel said.

"What if we didn't identify the real killer?" Alma asked. "Can you imagine the depressing results? How will we live with ourselves? Our credibility will be shredded to tatters."

"We'll cross that bridge when, and if, we come to it," Isabel replied.

"Sammi Jo, what do you think?" Alma asked. "Did Roscoe get it right? Is Farrah the killer we're so desperate to catch?"

"Ask me later because we've got a live one," Sammi Jo replied, her finger pointing out the windshield.

"What do you know? Jodie finally showed up," Isabel said. "She was starting to make me look bad by not coming back tonight."

"We know she works those long office hours," Sammi Jo said.

"With a bit of luck, we'll observe just what it is she does on her overtime," Isabel said.

The shiny red taillights and brake lights to Jodie's car--they recognized its boxy contours and yellowish chassis--flickered off where she parked it in the painted slot by the office building. The streetlamp illuminated her car. She sat for a few moments while she finished sending a text message or taking a phone call.

After winging out her car door, Jodie emerged, her savage features cloaked in semi-darkness. Using the key fob, she locked the car doors remotely. She ran on the balls of her feet from the car to the nearby warehouse where she edged her way inside it.

"What's Jodie up to now?" Sammi Jo asked.

"It's no good. I can tell you that much," Alma replied.

"Let's hustle before we lose sight of her," Isabel said.

"In this nice floral-print dress?" Alma was shaking her head. "I don't think so."

"What did you think we'd be doing out here?" Isabel asked. "Stargazing?"

"You said we'd conduct a stakeout," Alma replied. "Nobody said we'd also be tailing the suspect around the pitch dark lumberyard."

"You should come prepared for anything," Isabel said.

"I came prepared to argue with you about your dumb ideas," Alma said.

"Be brave, Alma," Sammi Jo said. "It should be a cakewalk into the warehouse."

"The crazy things I do in this line of work never cease to amaze me," Alma said.

They disembarked from the car, stole up to the door Jodie had left ajar, and entered the warehouse. The clean aromatic smell of the freshly milled lumber--cedar?--pervading the bottom floor reminded Isabel of the cotton candy sold at the town carnival. Alma reached back to close the door behind them.

"Wait. Don't shut it just yet," Isabel said. "Jodie will remember how she left it while she's exiting. We shouldn't advertise ourselves."

"I knew that. I was just testing to see if you brought your 'A' game," Alma said.

"Did I pass the test?" Isabel asked.

"As always, you did so with flying colors," Alma replied. "Where did Jodie go next?"

"I noticed she was carrying a tote bag filled with something upstairs," Sammi Jo replied.

"Shall we also take the stairs?" Isabel asked.

"No elevator or escalator is available," Alma replied.

"All right, you can be our guide, smarty-pants," Isabel said.

Once they cleared the top of the stairway, flickering yellow light at the far end of the second level drew them at a slow, hunched-over creep. They ducked in behind the eight-foot stacks of floor planks and peered over the top to spy on Jodie working by the illumination of her flashlight.

She'd hoisted up the lid to a low chest and was dumping the items from the tote bag she'd brought into it. Next, she straightened them up, stood over the low chest for a moment as if to admire it, and lowered the lid.

"Oops," Alma whispered. "I've got bad news."

"Now what?" Isabel asked.

"I forgot to mute my smartphone," Alma replied.

"Oh, for the love of Mike, do I have to remind you of everything to do?" Isabel asked.

"Maybe nobody will ring me," Alma said.

"I demand a new partner," Isabel said. "And sister."

"Tough noogies. You're stuck with yours truly," Alma said.

"*S-h-h-h,*" Isabel said.

Jodie was too obsessed with completing her task to hear their whispers. She darted back to the stairway, flew down the steps, and scampered through the warehouse door. They heard her crank up the car engine and accelerate off from the lumberyard, departing in the same direction from which she'd come.

"I bet you didn't think to bring a Maglite," Alma said.

"You're on, little sister," Isabel said. "How many bear claws are you willing to wager?"

"It's a sucker's play, Alma," Sammi Jo said. "No smart gumshoe leaves home without a Maglite, and we know Isabel is a smart gumshoe."

"Why don't you take out your Maglite, so we can see our way around?" Alma said.

Isabel flicked on the Maglite, and they inspected Jodie's chest.

"Her trousseau chest is built from cherry," Isabel said, examining the grain. "She probably had Archie's carpenters construct it. She's keeping it in here until she moves into a place with room for it."

"She's a glutton for punishment if she's getting remarried," Alma said.

"I've heard no rumors of her dating a fellow much less marrying him," Sammi Jo said.

"That's not why she has the chest," Isabel said. "Alma, flip up the lid, and we'll have a look."

Alma swung it up, and Isabel spotlighted its contents with the Maglite's circular beam. They were left gape-jawed and stunned. As the senior member, Isabel expressed their reaction.

"Shazam," she said before laughing at her corny interjection.

"Talk about your gobs of green," Alma said.

"Seeing so many banknotes wrapped in bundles is giving me an adrenaline rush," Sammi Jo said.

"Did we find the money Jodie has stolen from her boss?" Alma asked.

"We also just witnessed her making the latest deposit of her ill-gotten gains," Isabel replied.

"Doesn't Jodie know crime doesn't pay?" Alma picked up the tote bag Jodie had discarded, snapped it open, and snatched up a money bundle.

"What do you think you're doing?" Isabel asked.

"What does it look like I'm doing?" Alma replied. "I'm collecting our fair portion of the found loot, tax-free, of course."

"You can't do that," Isabel said.

"I don't see why not," Alma said. "It's like winning at bingo night or the Virginia lottery."

"Has doubling up on your meds caused you to act and talk so goofy?" Isabel said. "We've never taken stolen money."

"If we hadn't recovered the stolen money, it would still be missing," Alma said. "Clearly, we deserve a reward or a finders' fee."

"We're obligated to return all of it," Isabel said.

"Look, I had to stomp around in this grungy, dark warehouse tonight," Alma said. "I should get something for my time and trouble."

"I'm not holding a moral debate with you," Isabel said. "Big sister knows best. So, just put the money bundle back without any more fuss and bother."

"Sammi Jo, help me scoop up the money bundles to stuff into the tote bag," Alma said. "Ignore goody-two-shoes Isabel. She can never be happy no matter what good fortune falls into our laps."

"I'm not taking one red cent of the money Jodie ripped off and doesn't belong to me," Sammi Jo said.

"Huh?" Alma said.

"I'm saying I'm not a crook like Jodie is," Sammi Jo said. "You know we're better than that, Alma."

"Thank you for sticking up for your convictions, Sammi Jo," Isabel said.

"Oh, drats and double drats, then." Alma tossed aside the money bundle and tote bag. "I can't believe I'm listening to your namby-pamby advice."

"You did the right thing." Isabel patted Alma on the back. "Our reputation stays untarnished, and I'm so proud of you."

"You made your point so ease up." Alma closed the lid to the chest but not before taking a final lingering gaze at the money bundles and imagining what cool things (books, books, and more books!) she could buy with them. "Maybe I should get a new partner," Alma muttered.

Chapter 18

Isabel, Alma, and Sammi Jo sitting in a window booth at Eddy's Deli were so engrossed talking to their favorite server Tabitha they'd forgotten to order anything.

"I'm not surprised to hear you saw Jodie at the office tonight," Tabitha said. "She's a working fool, that girl is."

"Does she drop by for a bite to eat after she's finished putting in her long hours?" Sammi Jo asked.

"She usually pops in about fifteen minutes before our closing time," Tabitha replied. "It sends Eddy right up the wall, and I have to remind him we're obligated to serve our customers during all the posted hours."

"Does she sit and chew the rag with you?" Sammi Jo asked.

"We usually slow down near closing time, so I don't mind gabbing with the customers who are still here," Tabitha replied. "They're more interesting conversationalists than tired, grumpy Eddy is."

"What sort of gossip does Jodie bring up?" Sammi Jo asked.

"She gives me the lowdown on how things are going at the lumberyard," Tabitha replied. "We talk about employees and customers. Her boss Archie is fair game, too."

"She has Archie wrapped around her little finger," Sammi Jo said.

Tabitha laughed. "She's perky and funny, so I can see how Archie would like her. She single-handedly straightened out the financial mess in his office and rescued his business from tanking."

"Does she like to take credit for it?" Sammi Jo asked.

"Everybody says she did, and I've even heard Archie say it," Tabitha replied. "She happened along at the right time is what he tells us."

"If the boss man says you're good, then you must be good," Sammi Jo said.

Tabitha frowned at Sammi Jo. "I don't believe I like your sarcastic tone. Have you got something against Jodie?"

"Let me put it this way," Sammi Jo replied. "I wouldn't get too chummy with her if I were you. The you-know-what is about to hit the fan, and you don't want to be caught standing in front of it when it does."

Tabitha was miffed. "Well, I like Jodie fine. We're not best friends for life, but her banter makes me laugh, and she's a generous tipper."

"The last part doesn't amaze me," Sammi Jo said.

"Do you know where she stays in town?" Isabel asked.

"She's been boarding with Mrs. Brentwood," Tabitha replied. "When Jodie has saved up enough money, she's going to buy her own place and move into it."

"It shouldn't take her too long at the rate she's going," Sammi Jo said.

"Does Jodie ever talk about her job?" Isabel asked.

"I'm a waitress and not a bookkeeper," Tabitha replied. "So, I wouldn't understand her if she got into the details of what she does at the lumberyard office."

"She must be shaken up over the trauma of Laura's murder," Isabel said.

"I'm sure Jodie is although I haven't seen her come in since it happened," Tabitha said.

"She'll probably drop by shortly," Sammi Jo said. "We know she's putting in those fabulous work hours. Apparently, she's the only thing standing between Archie and bankruptcy."

"What's happened to you, Sammi Jo?" Tabitha asked. "I hope your snippy attitude improves soon. It doesn't become you."

Sammi Jo smiled. "I hope it does, too, before the night is done."

"I need to be off and take care of something before it gets too late," Isabel said.

"I'll tag along with you," Sammi Jo said. "Alma, are you coming?"

"Are you kidding? I wouldn't miss it for the world," Alma replied.

"Thanks a mint for chatting with us, Tabitha," Isabel said. "We'll drop by back for an early breakfast. See you then."

"Keep your saddle oiled and your gun greased," Tabitha said.

Isabel laughed.

Mrs. Brentwood was a town widow who resided in a white-shingled, two-story Colonial with green shutters. She'd rented out her spare upstairs bedrooms for more than a decade, starting right after her husband fell to his death through an exposed manhole. A retired schoolteacher, she carefully screened her female boarders, enforced her room agreements, and collected the weekly rent. She permitted no pets, no smoking, and no children on the premises. However, she offered her boarders generous kitchen privileges.

Isabel and Alma knew Mrs. Brentwood through their church. A moon-faced, red-haired, and small-framed lady, Mrs. Brentwood had a soft voice and a quick smile. She doted on an indoor Clumber spaniel she called Stinkerbell. She indicated Jodie was caught up on her rent. Then Isabel laid out what "small favor" they sought.

"Now, Isabel, you must realize I can't let you into Jodie's room without first obtaining her permission," Mrs. Brentwood said.

Isabel nodded. "I was afraid you might object, but this case involves the murder of Jodie's sister, Laura."

"I know you're like the plucky women sleuths I used to watch on the television programs." Mrs. Brentwood chuckled. "The Snoop Sisters were a riot, and I never missed watching an episode. Anyway, I can't let you invade my boarders' privacy, or I'll break the trust I've established with them."

Alma came up with a compromise. "Have you recently emptied the wastebasket in Jodie's room?"

"I did this morning while Stinkerbell and I were dusting and straightening up the place," Mrs. Brentwood replied.

"The trash Jodie set out means she relinquished any ownership of it," Alma replied. "We're legally in the clear to pick through it if we think it helps us."

Mrs. Brentwood's bemused expression didn't change. "If you wish to rummage through Jodie's trash, I guess it's okay with me."

"We came prepared to hunt for clues." Isabel scrounged around in her pocketbook, wrested out three pairs of purple latex gloves like the dentists wear, and distributed them to Alma and Sammi Jo.

"I can see you've done this stuff before," Mrs. Brentwood said.

"Uh-huh, but we don't make a practice of it," Alma said, stretching on the purple latex gloves.

Mrs. Brentwood had put the trash she'd collected from her boarders' rooms into the large plastic bag she left by the rear door. Isabel adjusted her half-moon reading glasses to ride on the tip of her nose. She untied the plastic bag, reached down into it, and removed the items one by one. After checking it, she handed it to Alma.

One of Mrs. Brentwood's boarders liked to solve the Sudoku puzzles in red ink while another fed a sweet tooth with chocolate candy bars. Mrs. Brentwood left with Stinkerbell to do something in the front room while they performed the unglamorous task. Before too long, Alma voiced her frustration and discontent.

"I doubt if Jessica Fletcher ever had to put on purple latex gloves and root through her murder suspects' trash," Alma said.

"She was a famous TV star making the big bucks, and we're not," Isabel said.

"It's nice work if you can get it," Alma said.

Isabel sighed.

"She makes it look so effortless and exciting on her TV program," Alma said. "Are you getting any closer to hitting pay dirt?"

"Gracious me, but you've turned into a fusspot," Isabel replied.

"Grumbling keeps me sane while I'm doing tedious stuff like this," Alma said.

Upstairs in the rented rooms, they heard a TV or radio blaring. Isabel mused over what the boarders, especially Jodie, did for their nightly entertainment. Did Mrs. Brentwood use a wireless router and offer free WiFi with the rent she charged? Had Jodie googled how she could pull off the perfect murder without getting caught? The open question of the murder weapon (Farrah's Indian club?) arose in Isabel's mind again.

"Can you give me a rough idea of what we're after?" Alma asked.

"We'll know we've found a clue when it burns our fingers," Isabel replied. "Here you go, take this."

Alma accepted the broken pink headband the joggers put on before embarking on their runs.

"Let your imagination run amok and tell me what clue would break Laura's murder case wide open," Isabel said after she smoothed out a crumpled-up slip of paper she'd removed.

"You just found a sales receipt, didn't you?" Alma said.

"Indeed, I did," Isabel replied.

"It probably goes to the diary Jodie bought and used to frame Deacon for Laura's murder," Alma said.

"Yes again," Isabel replied.

"Where did she make the purchase?" Alma asked.

"The sales receipt is from the five-and-dime in town," Isabel replied.

"We'll call Sheriff Fox to get over here," Alma said.

"Not quite yet," Isabel said.

"Then we'll hold on to the sales receipt," Alma said.

Isabel shook her head. "I'll stuff it back into the trash bag."

"Is doing that kosher?" Alma asked.

"Is anything we ever do as meddlers kosher?" Isabel replied.

"I can't speak for you, but I'm as kosher as a dill pickle taken straight out of the jar," Alma replied.

"That's funny because I've had a yen for a dill pickle," Sammi Jo said.

Alma gave Sammi Jo a droll glance. "Is there something you want to tell us? Did the family heirloom finally work its magical fertility powers on you?"

"No, Alma, I'm not pregnant as far as I know," Sammi Jo replied.

Mrs. Brentwood hurried into the back room, her eyes shining brightly.

"I glanced out the window and saw Jodie pulling up to the curb in her yellow car," Mrs. Brentwood said. "Are you sticking around?"

"We'd be caught in an awkward position if we did," Isabel replied.

"Then you should cut out the back door and alley, so Jodie doesn't cause any trouble," Mrs. Brentwood said.

"Set this trash bag aside," Isabel said, handing it to Mrs. Brentwood. "Whatever you do, please don't throw it away under any circumstances."

"Sure thing but I have to say you ladies sure are hung up on rooting through other folks' trash," Mrs. Brentwood said.

"We could say it goes with the territory," Isabel said, peeling off the purple latex gloves.

"It's dirty work, but somebody has to do it," Alma said. "This time it paid off for us."

For the second time that night, they huddled in the car parked on the dark side of the street. They'd set up outside of Mrs. Brentwood's house where Jodie was ensconced upstairs in her rented room. Isabel had no idea how they'd benefit from keeping vigil on Jodie, but they should stay busy doing something relevant to the murder case. Isabel and Sammi Jo kept their eyes peeled on the front door. However, Alma soon grew bored and took out her smartphone to swipe through its screens.

"Mrs. Brentwood might boot Jodie out tonight," Sammi Jo said.

"She said she won't interfere with our case," Isabel said. "I asked her."

"She won't tolerate having a possible killer sleeping under her roof for very long," Sammi Jo said.

"We only get the one bite of the apple," Alma said. "Let's do our best and not muck it up."

"We know the stakes couldn't be much higher," Isabel said.

"Maybe Jodie will get the munchies and make a quick trip out to Eddy's Deli or Fredo's Frozen Custard," Sammi Jo said.

"If I were Jodie, I'd slip into my comfy pajamas, settle in with a good book, and call for home delivery," Alma said. "Eddy delivers in town."

"How much stolen money do you figure Jodie has squirreled away in her treasure chest?" Sammi Jo asked.

"I planned to stay and count it, but Isabel was in such a hurry to leave," Alma replied.

"I didn't trust your sticky fingers to count it," Isabel said.

"The only time my fingers get sticky is after I eat a bear claw," Alma said.

"Jodie has been a busy little bee," Isabel said.

"I wonder how many of her previous employers she fleeced and got away with it," Alma said.

"Maybe Bernie caught wind of her thefts and divorced her before he was left holding the bag when she was convicted and went to prison," Isabel said.

"He should've blown the whistle if he knew she was doing something illegal," Alma said.

"All he wanted to do was to sever their ties for keeps," Alma said.

"Pay attention, all," Isabel said. "Somebody is coming out."

"Jodie has made her next appearance," Sammi Jo said, peering in the same direction. "She's dressed for a nighttime jog. Shall we join her and make it a foursome?"

"The last time I jogged anywhere is a distant memory," Isabel replied.

Jodie wore a pink running cap, pink running jersey, and pink running shorts. Her pink wristbands, pink fanny pack, and pink running shoes reflected the streetlights' brightness. All told, she was well equipped to take a nighttime jog when the temperature had cooled, and less traffic ran on the streets. She performed a few squats and lunges to stretch her leg muscles and took off jogging at a leisurely pace.

"How are we going to prowl along and follow her in our car?" Isabel asked.

"Why should we bother?" Alma replied. "We can see she's going for a run. Nothing else is left for us to see tonight. We can bag it and go home."

"Isn't Jodie a bit overdressed for the occasion?" Isabel asked. "She's put on everything she can think of to show everybody who happens to see her that she's a jogger."

"Then is she up to something else?" Alma asked.

"I'd like to know if she is or not," Isabel replied.

"She's disappearing from view," Alma said.

"I'll hop out and tail her on foot," Sammi Jo said. "Leave on your smartphones, and I'll call in with my updates on what I see her doing. How does my plan ring?"

"I give it my seal of approval," Isabel replied.

"If you get tired and can't keep up, take a short break and rest," Alma said.

Sammi Jo scoffed at the idea. "She's not in better physical shape than me. Besides, she's three or four years older, so I'm the young thing."

After Sammi Jo scrambled off to follow Jodie down the dark town streets, Isabel nodded out the windshield.

"Talk about your girl with moxie," Isabel said. "I'm glad Sammi Jo is on our side."

"You're preaching to the faithful," Alma said. "I knew it from the first day we met her. I said, 'Hey, Isabel, that Sammi Jo Garner is so full of moxie, it's coming out of her ears.'"

"You never uttered any such thing to me," Isabel said. "I was the first to note and remark on her moxie."

Alma did a harrumph. "Is your smartphone turned on?"

"Yes, I just checked it again," Isabel replied.

"Shall we move to a different spot?" Alma asked. "Some town busybody might get suspicious over how long we've been loitering here."

Isabel drove further down the street and eased over to park under a streetlight. She held her smartphone and pretended as if she was taking a call to give them a cover story for why they were stopped there.

"You suspect Jodie is using the disguise of a jogger," Alma said.

"The over-the-top way she's dressed strikes me as rather incongruous," Isabel said.

"Why is she using the disguise?" Alma asked.

"I don't have even the whiff of suspicion," Isabel replied.

Isabel's smartphone rang, and she put on her speakerphone.

"Guess where Jodie has gone?" Sammi Jo asked.

"Sorry, but I've sworn off making any guesses tonight," Isabel replied.

"She stopped at the hardware store," Sammi Jo said.

"Why does a nocturnal jogger need to purchase a box of six-penny nails or a plumber's helper?" Isabel asked.

"I wondered the same thing," Sammi Jo replied.

"Can you see what she's doing?" Isabel asked.

"Not without her catching a glimpse of me," Sammi Jo replied. "I'll duck in and get the scoop from Blaine after she leaves."

"She might give you the slip while you're with him," Isabel said. "Keep on shadowing her. We have to learn what she's doing out here tonight."

"She just exited the hardware store," Sammi Jo said.

"I'll let you go then," Isabel said. "Bye for now."

Isabel hung up while Alma stopped swiping the screens on her smartphone.

"It's just a thought, but what if Jodie is in cahoots with Farrah?" Alma asked. "Maybe they colluded and hatched the murder plot to kill Laura in the beauty shop."

"Our previous murder cases have taken surprising twists and turns," Isabel said. "However, I don't envision Jodie as a trusting soul who'd team up with a partner in crime like Farrah."

"Taking a partner would make it riskier to cover up the murder," Alma said. "What if the partner gets arrested and decides to flip, confessing everything in exchange for a lighter prison sentence?"

"Good point," Isabel said. "Have we ever faced partners in crime conspiring to murder a victim?"

Alma shook her head. "I don't think so."

"Then I'd say the possibility is a remote one this time," Isabel said.

The smartphone beckoned again, and Isabel communicated with Sammi Jo.

"Guess what's happened now," Sammi Jo said.

"The guesses are flying around tonight like Willie's UFOs," Isabel said.

Sammi Jo laughed. "Jodie has returned to the scene of the crime."

"What's she doing at Farrah's Beauty Shop?" Isabel asked.

"She just sneaked down the rear alley," Sammi Jo replied.

"Has she spotted you?" Isabel asked.

"Isabel, really now. Do you need to ask me that question?" Sammi Jo replied. "I can dog a murder suspect on foot with no complications."

"Then go on and tail Jodie into the rear alley," Isabel said.

"I'll watch her like a hawk," Sammi Jo said. "She won't sneeze without me knowing it."

"Alma and I are on our way," Isabel said. "Hold tight. We'll be there in a jiff."

"I'll hang loose until you show up," Sammi Jo said. "Wow, I can't believe how hard my heart is pounding."

Isabel chuckled with delight. "Don't you just love feeling it, too?"

Chapter 19

Isabel and Alma sat in the car parked on Main Street while Isabel scolded her phone caller.

"Roscoe Fox, I don't give a rat's patootie if you've gotten relaxed to watch *Baywatch* on DVD. You hop off your recliner and drag your lazybones on down to Farrah's Beauty Shop. Do I make myself crystal clear?"

"Why didn't you call Deputy Sheriff Bexley?" Sheriff Fox asked.

"Perhaps I should call your boss the mayor," Isabel replied.

"Why are you and Alma even there?" Sheriff Fox asked "I gave you the direct order to cease and desist your sleuthwork on the Laura Isherwood homicide. Now isn't it true?"

"We never pay any attention to your direct orders when they're ridiculous like that one," Isabel said. "Now climb onto your fastest horse and giddy-up."

"No ma'am," Sheriff Fox said.

"I beg your pardon?" Isabel asked.

"Are you hard of hearing?" Sheriff Fox replied. "I said no. I'm not running downtown to Farrah's Beauty Shop just because you think I should when you snap your fingers."

Isabel glanced at Alma. "Roscoe said he's a no-show. How do you like that?"

"We elected a do-nothing for our town sheriff," Alma replied. "Maybe our town will have better luck in the next election."

"I heard that wisecrack," Sheriff Fox said.

"The killer has already left one murder victim," Isabel said. "What's two more--you and I--for Sheriff Fox to investigate tomorrow morning when he gets the frantic phone call?"

"A triple homicide happening in our small town will churn up things," Alma replied. "The crime report will break on the major news outlets, and it may very well *go viral.*"

"Go viral?" Sheriff Fox repeated with the horror rising in his high-pitched voice. "I might lose my cushy job, and I can't afford to take the chance."

"Then you have five minutes to get down here," Isabel said.

"I have to get dressed, trim my toenails, and floss my teeth," Sheriff Fox said.

"There isn't enough time," Isabel said. "Just come as you are."

"My police cruiser needs a tank of gas," Sheriff Fox said.

"Are you trying to make me lose it and scream like a madwoman?" Isabel asked.

"All right, I'm coming. Don't touch anything or do anything until I get there," Sheriff Fox replied. "I'll take charge when I arrive on the scene."

"Thanks for the timely reminder," Isabel said. "I'd almost forgotten."

After they disconnected, Alma asked Isabel, "Were you serious about us waiting for Sheriff Fox?"

Isabel just laughed. "Shall we go see what Sammi Jo has cooking?" she said.

Isabel, Alma, and Sammi Jo crouched down behind the half-full trash dumpster in the rear alleyway to Farrah's Beauty Shop. They hid a stone's toss away from the door. The exterior light she had installed created a well-lit space.

"After a lot of fumbling around, Jodie was able to pick the door lock," Sammi Jo said. "I've been watching it ever since, and she never came back out."

"Why did she go inside?" Alma asked. "Sheriff Fox has gone over the crime scene with a fine-toothed comb."

"I don't have the foggiest idea how her warped mind works," Isabel replied.

"Sheriff Fox is en route," Alma said. "Isabel browbeat him into it."

"He grumbled it's past his quitting time, and he's all comfy for bed," Isabel said with disgust. "He acted as if rounding up the killer wasn't his responsibility. Did he expect us to arrest him?"

"The important thing is he's on his way," Sammi Jo said.

"We should do something to prevent Jodie from getting away," Isabel said.

"You're our fearless leader, so you can lead us," Alma said.

"We muddle through it again in our grand fashion," Isabel said.

They emerged from behind the trash dumpster and drew up to the alleyway door. Isabel tried the doorknob. It didn't twist. She frowned. Again, she turned it with no better luck.

"Is it locked?" Alma asked.

"No, Alma. I get my jollies by chatting with you in a dark alleyway," Isabel replied.

"Do sarcastic remarks now unlock doors?" Alma said.

"You asked me a goofy question," Isabel said.

"Are you calling me goofy?" Alma asked.

"Okay, let's all take a deep breath," Sammi Jo said. "If Jodie figured it out, we can do it, too."

"Did you bring a lock pick kit?" Isabel asked.

"Perhaps I did," Alma replied. "Shall I search in my pocketbook?"

"Please spare us from going through that ordeal again," Isabel replied.

"Didn't I see you have a butter knife?" Sammi Jo asked.

"I carry one although I don't recall why," Alma replied.

"You probably swiped it from Eddy's Deli," Isabel said.

"Sammi Jo, Isabel is busting my chops again," Alma said.

"Lend it to me," Sammi Jo said. "Maybe I can insert it to jimmy the spring-bolt lock." With a few wiggles, she accomplished just that.

"Nancy Drew did the same thing," Alma said.

"So has every other TV detective except they use a credit card," Isabel said.

They crept through the alleyway door into the rear part of the beauty shop smelling of warm blown-dry hair and musky shampoo fragrance. Everything lay still and quiet. They skulked past the break room and into the ill-lit work area. The station mirrors and salon styling chairs were set up for opening tomorrow morning. The only thing out of place was Jodie clad in her pink jogging apparel.

She squatted on the floor in front of Farrah's grandfather clock. The lower pendulum door, a beveled glass panel, was open to access the clock case. The heavy pendulum rod and bob constructed of brass no longer swung back and forth behind the three weight canisters dangling on clock chains.

Clever with her hands, Jodie had carefully detached it. She was wiping it down with the cotton balls she'd stuffed into her pink fanny pack. The fumes of isopropyl alcohol permeated the room. During her "jog," she'd purchased a container of isopropyl alcohol and a bag of cotton balls from Blaine at the hardware store. She'd discarded several used cotton balls, and her fanny pack was unzipped.

Scrubbing away with a determined fury, Jodie's concentration centered on carrying out her cleanup mission. She flipped the hair out of her eyes before she examined her progress in the stronger light. Cursing in dismay, she resumed her feverish scouring. She failed to realize she had three visitors.

"Why, hello there, Jodie," Isabel said. "Fancy meeting you here at this late hour."

Jerking up her head, Jodie hissed in surprise. Her eyes slitted like a giant cat as her tense body trembled.

"You three are pests," she said. "How did you get in here?"

"The alleyway door also opens for us," Isabel replied.

"How? I locked it," Jodie said.

"One summer I worked at the locks counter at a home improvement store," Sammi Jo replied. "I tripped this door lock as easily as you did."

"What are you so busy doing?" Isabel asked.

"It's none of your business," Jodie replied.

"Are you removing Laura's bloodstain from the murder weapon?" Isabel asked. "Are you fearful we'll zero in on how you murdered Laura?"

Jodie glanced down at the heavy pendulum rod and bob she clutched in her white knuckles. She sized up her visitors, gauging her chances of evading them and exiting the alleyway door. Her freedom was so close. She gripped the heavy pendulum rod and bob, poising to spring up and swing it again.

Sammi Jo, divining Jodie's plan, took a step sideways, blocking her escape route to the alleyway door.

"Even if you're armed, you won't get by me," Sammi Jo said. "Trust me."

"Why are you harassing me?" Jodie asked, relaxing a little.

"We've had our suspicions all along," Sammi Jo replied. "As it turns out, they're spot-on."

"What are you talking about?" Jodie asked.

"It's not complicated," Isabel replied. "Did you kill Laura?"

"You have no legal standing to confront me with that outrageous accusation," Jodie replied.

"They don't, but I do." Sheriff Fox stepped up into the brighter light. He'd pinned on the sheriff's badge to the breast pocket of his monogrammed--"RF"--seersucker bathrobe worn over his pinstriped pajamas and taupe suede slippers. He'd belted the holster with his service weapon around his wide girth. His Smokey Bear uniform hat covered his bald spot. Isabel wanted to laugh, but since he'd done as she'd asked, she couldn't very well mock him.

"What's going on here?" Jodie asked.

"Slowly put down and let go of the clock pendulum," Sheriff Fox replied. "We can talk about it, but not until you're secured in handcuffs."

Seeing she'd run out of options and clenching her teeth, Jodie set aside the heavy pendulum rod and bob.

"Are you charging me with a crime?" Jodie asked.

"*Crimes*," Isabel replied. "Murder and embezzlement are the first two crimes we know about and can prove."

"Embezzlement, eh?" Sheriff Fox pulled Jodie up to her feet and subdued her in a pair of handcuffs. "That's a new one on me. Give me the short version."

"Jodie has been siphoning off money from Archie Blevins and storing it in a trousseau chest made of cherry," Isabel said. "You can recover it inside the lumberyard warehouse on the second floor at the far end behind the stacks of floor planks."

"Embezzlement is also a major crime," Sheriff Fox said. "Thank goodness I arrived as soon as I did."

"You show up in the nick of time," Alma said. "We thank our lucky stars you're our town sheriff."

"I appreciate hearing your support even if I detect the hint of sarcasm," Sheriff Fox said.

"Jodie, how did Laura learn you were embezzling from Archie?" Isabel asked.

Letting out an exasperated sigh, Jodie knew she'd reached the end of the line. She drew in a breath and described the accidental way her lucrative caper had come unraveled.

"I drove when Laura and I went clothes shopping at the mall," Jodie said. "I'd forgotten to put on my sunglasses, so I distractedly asked her to dig them out of my purse. She reached back and grabbed my purse. While scrounging through my stuff, she came across my expensive piece of jewelry crusted with diamonds, rubies, and emeralds. She freaked out since she knew I couldn't afford it on my salary and credit history. She asked me too many questions. I tried to spin her that it was a fake bauble, but sisters as close as we were can see through it. She wouldn't let it go, no matter how much I cajoled her."

"What did she expect you to do?" Isabel asked.

"She turned self-righteous and urged me to turn myself in and come clean." Jodie laughed in a vulgar manner. "I'd just say a few rosaries for penance, and the law would forgive and forget my crime. Only my naive, gullible kid sister would think like that."

"You sneaked in early through the alleyway door like you did tonight, hid in the break room, and ambushed Laura right after she entered the beauty shop," Isabel said. "Am I on the right track?"

"I killed Laura by striking her in the temple with the clock pendulum," Jodie said as calmly as if she was giving the day's weather. "I was surprised by how little force it took me on the first swat."

Isabel looked at Sheriff Fox who nodded. He'd witnessed Jodie's murder confession.

"You forged the entries in Laura's bogus diary," Isabel said. "You planted it in the townhouse she'd rented to incriminate Deacon for her murder. You knew they'd been squabbling, and it provided you with a handy motive to hang on him."

"I knew enough details about their marital discord to make the diary entries point the finger of suspicion at him," Jodie said. "My and Laura's handwriting looks practically identical."

"We showed your forged diary to Deacon," Isabel said as she gave it to Sheriff Fox. "He pointed out the glaring inaccuracies you made and proved to us it's a counterfeit."

"What Laura ever saw in him is beyond me," Jodie said.

"Did she like to confide in you?" Isabel asked.

"We talked almost daily in person or over the phone," Jodie replied. "She wanted to leave him and make it on her own for the first time. They'd been married since she was sixteen, and she craved her independence. I did what I could to support and bolster her."

"You did up until the day she discovered you were stealing cash hand over fist from your employer," Isabel said.

Jodie shrugged as best she was able to while tethered in a pair of handcuffs. "Laura didn't--couldn't--understand how the real world works, how you get ahead by doing what you have to do even if it means getting down and dirty."

"We contacted your ex in Richmond," Isabel said. "Bernie provided us with insights about your reckless spending habits."

"Bernie Wright." Making a baleful face, Jodie said it with bitter disdain. "How did I ever marry a tree surgeon? What a loser and sucker."

"Bernie isn't headed to prison for a long time," Isabel said. "You are."

Jodie said nothing.

"How convenient your customers paid you in cash, and you made your daily bank trips to deposit at least some of the money," Isabel said. "The rest of it went into your money chest."

"I figured why not take advantage of Archie's lax oversight," Jodie said. "He didn't use the proper checks and balances. As the Good Book says, a fool and his money are soon parted."

"A fool commits murder, figuring she'll be canny enough to get away with it," Isabel said.

"I killed Laura only because I had no other choice," Jodie said.

"What did she tell you before she died?" Isabel asked.

"She said that she'd forgive me," Jodie replied. "I just laughed."

"You can have the last word on the matter," Isabel said.

"We've kicked things around enough for one night," Sheriff Fox said. "I have a pile of paperwork to finish before I can go home, thanks to my favorite lady sleuths."

"As always, you're quite welcome, Roscoe," Isabel said. "Alma and Sammi Jo, our work here is finished, as they say. Shall we go home?"

Chapter 20

"Eddy says breakfast is on the house, ladies," Tabitha said. "We feel it's the least we can do to say thanks for solving the murder."

"My horoscope predicted today is my lucky day," Alma said, smiling. "Okay, I'll start with a chocolate-drizzled bear claw, and the biggest, juiciest maraschino cherry you have centered on the tippy top."

Tabitha scribbled it down on her order pad. She glanced at the scowling Isabel who sat in the opposite seat at the window booth.

"I'm tempted to devour one of those scrumptious Alma Specials later on," Tabitha said. "What's your dining pleasure, Isabel? Have you got a sweet tooth like Alma?"

"I'll exercise my older sister's veto powers and cancel Alma's order," Isabel said. "We never eat chocolate-drizzled bear claws for breakfast, or at any other time for that matter."

"I need to keep my energy level up to function at my peak mental capacity," Alma said.

"You have more than enough energy as it is," Isabel said.

"What if I bring out your usual breakfast orders?" Tabitha asked. "Does my idea appeal to you?"

"You make a capital suggestion," Isabel replied.

"Yeah, it's good by me, too," Alma said.

Tabitha left them and returned to the kitchen.

"When is Sammi Jo coming inside with us?" Alma asked.

"She'll wind up her phone call here directly." Isabel could see an exasperated Sammi Jo through the diner window gesticulating with her hand and speaking forcefully. "Have a little patience and don't grumble at her."

"What's keeping her?" Alma asked. "We had to start our breakfast without her placing her order. Shall I go out and grab her?"

"She and Reynolds are discussing their wedding date," Isabel replied.

Alma raised her eyebrows. "Is Reynolds going through with it this time?"

Isabel held up her hands. "I'm keeping all my fingers crossed he will do the right thing."

"Thank our lucky stars Farrah opened up this morning and is back in business," Alma said.

"Your new hairdo looks smashing, and I'm so green with envy," Isabel said.

"Your hair appointment is this afternoon," Alma said. "You'll come out of Farrah's Beauty Shop looking every bit as smashing as I do."

"Did she say if Sheriff Fox returned the Indian club to her?" Isabel asked.

"He did through Deputy Sheriff Bexley, and she took it home," Alma replied. "She brought it to work to show one of her hairstylists."

"Did she get her grandfather clock back up and running?" Isabel asked.

"She paid a clockmaker to fix it and replace the pendulum," Alma replied. "It keeps perfect time now, and she's over the moon."

"Farrah is a lot like us," Isabel said. "It doesn't take a lot to make her happy."

"Speak for yourself--I didn't get my chocolate-drizzled bear claw," Alma said.

"What did Blaine say when he called you this morning?" Isabel asked.

"Deacon switched off the TV, put away his playing cards, and headed back to work operating the forklift," Alma replied. "He and Blaine are leaving for a week to camp out and trout fish up in the Blue Ridge Mountains."

"I'm sure Deacon will benefit immensely from it," Isabel said. "Sammi Jo just stepped through the doorway."

"It's about time," Alma said. "I'm growing faint from hunger."

"Oh, please, stop it. You're healthy as a horse," Isabel said.

Sammi Jo flopped down beside Alma who'd scooted over on the booth seat.

"Your glower on a bright sunny morning can only mean you've hit another snag in making your wedding plans," Isabel said.

"That man--Mr. Reynolds Kyle--can't decide to save his life." Sammi Jo folded her arms on her chest. "I'm left riding on a merry-go-round with him that never stops. What am I going to do?"

"Just hang on tight and keep riding it," Isabel replied.

"How does your suggestion help Sammi Jo?" Alma asked.

"What other choice does she have?" Isabel replied. "If she wants to get married to Reynolds, she has to keep riding his merry-go-round until it stops."

"What's happened now?" Alma asked.

"Where is Tabitha?" Sammi Jo looked around the diner. "I need a piping hot cup of coffee."

"She's back in the kitchen supervising Eddy," Isabel replied.

"Anyway, Reynolds finally dragged his sorry self home from the Darlington Raceway early this morning," Sammi Jo said. "He's always the last dog to leave the party."

"Didn't he leave it with you that he'd settled on a wedding date?" Isabel asked.

"I was preoccupied squaring away our murder case when he told me, and then he just as promptly forgot it," Sammi Jo replied.

"Next time grab his offer when he makes it," Isabel said. "He easily forgets his promises, and couples in love shouldn't do that."

"Force him to take a blood oath," Alma said. "Nobody forgets one of those."

"Ordinarily, I'd say Alma's suggestion is outlandish and impractical," Isabel said. "However at this juncture, I feel we're desperate enough to give anything a try."

"When is he going to learn to just go along and keep quiet about your wedding plans?" Alma asked.

"Any discussion of Reynolds Kyle is wasted breath," Sammi Jo replied. "What are your plans for today?"

"We're headed down to Brandy Station to see a woman named Quillie Custalow about her gorgeous winter quilts," Isabel replied. "She sews them by hand, and she has an artistic eye for capturing rural life and culture."

"With it ninety-plus in the shade, checking out winter quilts is odd, but we'd each like to purchase one before the autumn chill sets in," Alma said.

"Are her quilt prices reasonable?" Sammi Jo asked.

"For the most part, they're in line with the other quilts we've seen for sale," Isabel replied.

"If you don't have anything going on, come along with us," Alma said. "We'll stop for lunch at a diner we like. Their barbecued pulled pork sandwiches and creamy coleslaw made from scratch are out-of-this-world delicious."

"Is Petey Sampson going with you?" Sammi Jo asked.

"We'll have to see," Alma replied. "He's taking a siesta at home right now."

"You should count me in," Sammi Jo said.

"I'm already anticipating lunch, and I haven't eaten breakfast," Alma said.

"Alma, you're nothing but a foodie mess," Isabel said.

"What's wrong with enjoying my cuisine experiences?" Alma asked.

"How is Sheriff Fox?" Sammi Jo asked. "He must be quite proud of himself."

"He's all in a dither," Isabel replied. "I told him Louise and Megan are coming for a weekend visit."

"Handling all three Trumbo sisters at once is a lot to cope with," Alma said.

"I hope he survives it without blowing his mind," Sammi Jo said.

"Archie Blevins' carpenters are making us each a walnut quilt rack," Isabel said.

"Did he recover his stolen money Jodie kept in her trousseau chest?" Sammi Jo asked.

"Archie found it in the warehouse and claims he isn't short by one dime," Isabel replied.

"I find it difficult to believe," Alma said. "Jodie told us she spent a wad of the money on the piece of jewelry that Laura found in her pocketbook."

"He probably doesn't know how much money Jodie took and said it to make himself feel better," Sammi Jo said. "Since Archie needs an honest bookkeeper, I'll recommend my friend Alicia who just got laid off."

"Laura's murder is tough to understand much less accept," Isabel said. "All I did was toss and turn while lying in bed and mulling it over last night. Even the three snorts from Uncle Jimbo's brown jug didn't bring me any measure of peace."

"I'd offer you my comforting advice if I could," Alma said. "The trouble is I didn't do any better with getting my sleep. Sisters killing sisters over greed is unsettling, and I know I'll never get over it entirely."

"What do you think will happen to Jodie?" Sammi Jo asked.

"I'm not a lawyer," Isabel replied. "She might cop a guilty plea to murdering Laura in exchange for the prosecution not asking for the death penalty. There'll be no trial, and no evidence like the fake diary introduced. The judge will impose her prison sentence, probably life without parole."

"Why did Jodie use her trousseau chest to hide her loot?" Sammi Jo asked.

"She didn't want to leave a paper or electronic trail like putting it in a bank account," Isabel replied. "Or that's my layperson's theory."

"How long could she have gone on stealing from Archie before he realized it?" Sammi Jo asked.

"If Laura hadn't discovered Jodie's embezzlement by accident, she could've done it for as long as she wished," Isabel replied. "Since Archie didn't pay close attention, and he was a sucker for her glib talk, he would've never caught on to how she was a crook."

"The shame of it is Archie was paying her a good salary by Quiet Anchorage standards," Alma said.

"Hopefully, he profits from his mistakes and won't repeat them," Isabel said.

"It's all so hideous," Alma said.

"Even if, we stand ready in case somebody else comes to us and needs our assistance," Isabel said.

"We always leave the porch light turned on," Alma said.

"Oh good, Tabitha is on her way back from the kitchen," Isabel said, looking behind Alma and Sammi Jo.

"If you want to order anything, run it by Isabel first," Alma said to Sammi Jo. "She's screening our menu selections now."

Isabel smiled. "Tabitha has your chocolate-drizzled bear claw with the maraschino cherry centered on the tippy top. I nodded with a wink, so she knew I was teasing you when I told her to cancel it."

"It's not nice to kid around about my breakfast," Alma said. "Is our big Scrabble game still a go for tonight? Are the Three Musketeers still our guests? Is Sammi Jo also coming?"

"I'll take a rain check since I have boyfriend issues to square away," Sammi Jo replied.

"Willie has confirmed they'll be there with bells on their toes," Isabel said.

Everybody laughed. Everything was back to quiet in Quiet Anchorage, Virginia. For now, anyway.

The End